Plan B

a novel

Patricia J. Parsons

Moonlight Press | Toronto

ISBN: 978-0-9685456-8-3

The Headlines

Change Your Shoes, Change Your Life,

Avoiding a Fate Worse than Death: Or Why It's Better to be a Bag Lady Than Move Home to Your Parents' Basement

Your Ultimate Guide to 'Boomeranging': Or How to Return to the Nest and Keep Your Dignity

Is Facebook Ruining Your 'Real' Life?

Friends with Money: Just Watch Those Relationships Change

Curiosity Killed the Cat: When Nosiness Leads You Astray

When Your Friends Surprise You

Why Everyone is Blogging and Why You Should Consider Stepping Away from the Computer

How to Negotiate Your Way to Anything You Want

A Field Guide to Travel Prep: An Online Shopping Extravaganza!

How to be a 'Good' Tourist

Genius or Insanity: Finding that Fine Line

The Authentic Travel Experience: Not All It's Cracked Up To Be

Dream Trips You Didn't See Coming

Does a New Life Really Begin at the End of Your Comfort Zone?

Why the 'Active' Vacation Might Not Live up to its Press

Coffee: The Most Important Meal of the Day

How to Know When You're in Love...and the Science to Prove It

Uncertainty: The Essence of Romance

When Life Gives You Reality, it's Time to 'Get Real'

How to Declutter Your Life

How to Change the World: Or at Least Your Own World

Putting on Your 'Big-Girl' Panties Might be the Best Thing you ever Did

About the Author

Other Books by P.J.Parsons

*"...And the trouble is if you don't risk
anything, you risk even more...*

~ Isadora Wing in **Fear of Flying** by Erica Jong

Change Your Shoes, Change Your Life

I can't be exactly sure when I seriously began to see my life as a series of magazine articles. But the unmistakable truth is that at some point over the past few years, one after the other, their titles began to march across the pages of my mind. I can almost hear the rustling of the pages as one turns into another, and the catchy headlines lure me onward.

"Live Your Best Life" shouts at me from the rack. Then it melts into "Lose that Belly Fat: *Now!*" And then, one of my personal (and recurring) favourites, "Find the Secret to Happiness." Imagine! A secret to happiness? Who could write that kind of drivel to mess up young women's minds? To tell you the truth...I can...and I did. That was up until – well, it was up until I didn't. In fact, if someone would actually pay me to do it, I'd run out of this room and immediately write another article called "You Can Never Go Home: How to Avoid Becoming a Boomerang Kid." I have research material in spades now: that's the kind of material that makes lifestyle writers like me drool. But I'm getting ahead of myself. Perhaps it would help you if I started at the beginning.

My name is Jenn Postman, and I am a magazine junkie. I am seriously addicted. This kind of declaration is important. I learned this while researching an article on the twelve-step approach to freeing yourself of your love addiction. (I know – not very high-brow, but I didn't say I wrote literary fiction. Fiction, it might be, but literary? Not in the slightest.) Back to the magazine addiction.

There is just something about that glossy cover winking at me from the magazine stand at the grocery store, the book store, the newsstand—it crooks its metaphorical finger, draws me close. Once I get a whiff of those fragrance inserts, I've lost all control of my rational mind, and you just can't get those fragrances from the tablet or online editions. Never mind that the cover price of that fat September issue might be twelve dollars, and that might be the last twelve dollars in my wallet (something that has happened on more than one occasion through my poor student days and more recently, but I'm getting ahead of myself again). We're talking serious addiction here, and it's been my burden ever since I was introduced to the wonders of *Seventeen* magazine by my best friend Faith when we were all of eleven years old. She was the first one in my small circle of friends to decide that we needed lipstick—and it had to be pink—and I was happy to go along with my glamorous friend with the long blonde hair who had only to flash those bright white teeth at any boy she fancied, and he was hers.

Then I graduated to *Glamour* magazine and *Cosmopolitan*— *Cosmo*, as we liked to call it back before the word 'cosmo,' had a different and equally addictive meaning. Then, my development as a serious magazine addict began to stagnate as I tried to wrestle myself away from *Cosmo* and on to something more sophisticated—like *Vogue*. There was, however, something about *Cosmo* girls that made them different. Could it have been the boobs? Could it have been that I identified more with the *Cosmo* girls and their breasts than the androgynous, long-legged mannequins that seemed to populate the pages of *Vogue* magazine? It has to be said that these thoughts came long before I began to appreciate that the appearance of sophistication that oozed from the pages of *Vogue* was more suited to me personally. That was before I started my love affair with expensive clothes and long before I finished my Master's thesis in English literature and fancied myself a serious writer. Of course, my magazine addiction branched out to encompass other genres like the travel magazines and even the *New Yorker* (although the fact that it's published weekly meant that if I didn't keep up with my reading, the piles of magazines would inch ever higher, spilling out of the wicker baskets that I had strategically placed in my bedroom to catch them).

I can hear all of those academic types huffing at me right about now—what kind of a serious writer ends up as a 'lifestyle' writer for a middle-market women's magazine? My answer is simple: the kind of writer who actually prefers writing to serving up a grandé iced sugar-free caramel low-fat macchiato and calling herself a barista while waiting for David Remnick (of the *New Yorker*) to call. I'm a writer who took the first job on offer out of grad school after twenty-four applications, eleven writing samples and three interviews. I'm a writer whose first choice job was working for the *New Yorker*, but who realized that writing for *Vivacity Magazine (for women with verve, style and a life!)* was a foot in the door, not to mention that they were the only one that offered to take me on. Never mind that the editor was well known for her oddities—not in the style of *The Devil Wears Prada* kind of editor—more for a genuine quirkiness and a worldview that suggested that if we just all took our lingerie and cuticles more seriously, world peace would surely follow. But who am I to argue?

I was 24 years old and desperate for an income to pay off my grad school debt and buy a wardrobe. I was not aware until the moment that I walked into the loft-style offices in an odd brick building just off Adelaide West in downtown Toronto that I was, in fact, desperate for a real manicure and a pair of Jimmy Choo shoes. The problem was that I couldn't afford to buy even one of his shoes, much less a pair.

So, when Eleanor Sawchuck peered at me over her rhinestone-studded (if-I-have-to-wear-them-they-might-as-well-make-a- statement) reading glasses and tilted her head to the left, I sat there hoping that she would hire me. The ad said they were searching for a lifestyle writer. Well, I could write and had life...style...sort of. What more would you need for this?

"Jenn," she said, "I may call you Jenn, of course?"

I nodded. Of course, she could. It wasn't a question so much as a statement of her decision.

3

"Jenn," she continued, "I think that with a bit of work you might do well here with us. I do need a lifestyle writer, and it appears that you have more command of the English language than your average university graduate these days." She picked up my writing samples off her desk and scrutinized them. "I cannot for the life of me figure out what they teach in those ivory towers these days. Every girl who comes in here is practically illiterate, and they all have the most appalling nail beds."

I glanced surreptitiously at my nail beds that were folded in my lap, although perhaps I wasn't furtive enough. I think she noticed me looking. It wasn't a professional manicure, but at least I'd had the presence of mind to do my nails before setting out on an interview with the editor of a women's magazine whose monthly cover featured someone whom the editor (I supposed it was the editor anyway) considered the quintessence of the whole woman – the woman who was successful on her own terms, had a sense of her own style and had impeccable cuticles. I had done my homework. I knew that *Vivacity* was not quite in the league of *Vogue*, but there would be no sackcloth around the office; of that, I was sure. It turned out I was right. I was also surprised at the sense of professionalism and self-confidence that seemed to emanate from most of the other young women I saw that day. It seemed that Eleanor's unusual tendencies might actually be good for her protégées. So, when she offered me a paid internship, I knew I was off to the races. I could barely afford the rent on the tiny studio I found tucked into the attic of a renovated mansion on Jarvis Street. I took it over the protestations of my father, who, although he lived just shy of 2000 kilometres away, was aware of the reputation of that part of Toronto – not a good one. After six months, however, I was promoted to assistant lifestyle writer, and things began to look up. I moved into a tony one-bedroom in a new high-rise one street over and made good use of the swimming pool, gym and concierge. This was a godsend when my online shopping habit heated up.

I'll always believe that my elevation at *Vivacity* magazine was a result of a particular piece that I was assigned to write.

"Jenn," Eleanor said, coming up behind me in my tiny cubicle one morning at about the five-and-a-half-month mark of my internship. "Jenn, sweetie, I have this wonderful assignment for you. I want you to write a piece about lifestyle enhancements of the six-way dress." She said this with a straight face.

"Excuse me?"

"The six-way dress," she said, thrusting a flat, rectangular box at me. "Of course, you're aware of their impact. We've all been following their impact on this year's collections, and now Babbette has sent us one of hers. The fabric is divine!" She rolled her eyes heavenward.

She was referring to Babbette Gagné, a Quebecois designer known for her 'organic' approach to clothing, whatever that meant. I knew better than to open my mouth and say that, though. I also knew to avoid voicing the other thought that was flitting across my mind at that point. *On what planet*, I wanted to say, *did a dress that could be worn in six different ways constitute a lifestyle piece?* But I had learned my lesson the hard way the first month that I was there: that would be on the planet where the person to whom the assignment was given was also tasked with finding a way to make it fit within her area. In my case, anything could be made into a lifestyle piece—it was all a matter of creative spin, and I was becoming the queen of that spin.

She was so excited that I could hardly do anything else other than take the box that was now perilously close to decapitating me and going off to research and write. What precisely, I wondered, would constitute research for a lifestyle informed by wearing a particular piece of clothing?

"I'll take this home with me this weekend," I said, maneuvering the large box under my desk. After all, it was Friday afternoon.

"Don't you want to open it up right away so you can feel the fabric and begin to reflect on it?" Eleanor asked, removing her glasses and hanging them on the thick, solid gold necklace that was as much her trademark as the sparkly reading glasses.

"Babbette does marvellous work." The "marvellous" part came out as a kind of languorous drawl.

"I'm kind of in the middle of something," I said, nodding toward my computer screen. "I think that I'll be able to do the piece more justice if I could really take my time and just *focus*."

It was imperative to emphasize the concept of focus since that was one of Eleanor's pet projects: getting everyone to focus on one thing at a time. She totally thought that multi-tasking meant not doing anything well—needless to say, texting or tweeting, or even surreptitiously checking emails during staff meetings, was *verboten*. She was constantly emailing us little *bon mots* and references about how to focus better. She also often included links to the latest research indicating that there is no such thing as being able to multi-task—all we were doing was switch-tasking, and evidently not very well.

"I could open it up while I'm alone and contemplate it in solitude," I said solemnly.

Eleanor nodded, smiling knowingly at me. In addition to her emphasis on being able to focus on one thing at a time, she was a big believer in meditative approaches to solving problems and coming up with innovative ideas. "I'll check in with you at the beginning of next week, then." She was beaming and humming to herself as she made her way back through the cubicles to her corner office with the sheepskin rug and the cashmere pillows, all compliments of a *feng shui* piece that we had recently run.

Taking the box home with me that evening, I wondered whether this would be a one or two-glass assignment. Wine, that is. By the time I decided to bring in the reinforcements later that evening, I was on my third glass of carménère and was starting to get a bit giddy trying to follow the instructions that came with the dress. Imagine clothing that needed instructions just to figure out how to put it on! As if life were not complicated enough.

The instructions consisted of a series of six line drawings of a stick figure with the thing wrapped around it in various ways. I picked up the dress—if you could call it that—from the box and had to admit that at least it felt nice. The fabric was a kind of silky jersey in a deep emerald green. I rubbed it against my face, barely avoiding knocking over my large balloon glass of deep, dark red wine on it. Dear god, I thought, I'll have to be more careful. Don't want to waste a single drop of wine. I was going to need every last one to get this article written. So, I picked up my cell phone and tapped Matt's photo, all the while still caressing the dress, which, just as Eleanor had predicted, was of a phenomenally soft fabric, a bit like caressing cotton candy. Back to Matt.

I adore Matt. He is, without a doubt, the perfect man—sort of. He has been my very best friend since my first year in university when he and his boyfriend had taken me under their collective wing. They helped me find my way around campus after I bumped into them (literally), spilling a cup of iced coffee all over Matt's suede blazer. I was mortified, but they were both good-humoured about it. Of course, the boyfriend part is what makes Matt only "sort of" perfect. Matthew Grey (he probably had fifty shades long before that Christian Grey guy emerged on paper and screen) is tall, handsome, and has a dazzling smile and dark, thick hair that sometimes falls adorably onto his forehead when he's concentrating. And his sense of style is impeccable: he always knows exactly what to wear for what occasion and how to wear it. But, of course, you've already guessed it – just like all the other fabulous single men out there these days, he's gay. But then, if he were not gay, we'd be a thing, and I wouldn't have my best friend, would I?

When Matt graduated and went off to law school at the end of my second year, I was almost despondent, but he was the one who encouraged me to go on to get my Master's degree and to follow my passion to be a writer. Oddly enough, he had been passionate about the law since he was eight years old! I had never met a child that young who wanted to be a lawyer, but then I came from a tiny seaside town where the main passions run to two extremes: finding a way to eke out a living somehow so that you never have to set foot outside the town limits, or trying with all your might to get out and never go back. I'm afraid I fell into the latter category.

I knew that it would be hopeless to call Andrew, the actual boyfriend of the moment. I had met him after spilling yet another drink—this time a Cosmo—all over him at a bar one night during my first week on the job at *Vivacity* when I was out celebrating having actually landed a paying job. I never seem to spill drinks on anyone else other than men, and usually on men I am trying to impress. I think there might be a lifestyle article in there somewhere. Anyway, although he and I had been dating for five months at the point when I was trying to make a lifestyle piece out of a hideous dress, we had never managed to spend a single Friday night together. He always worked until almost midnight, after which he was so exhausted from doing that every day of the workweek that he would head to his own apartment and crash. When he'd come up for air on Saturday afternoons, he would call. Well, at least he always said he was working. I chose to believe him because I'm not the sort to check.

Despite his American Ivy League MBA, Andrew had the misfortune of being just one step above the janitor (at least I think he was above the janitor) with a big investment bank on Bay Street, where the only piece of art in the waiting room was a huge, framed poster from one of those motivational products companies. It was a picture of an enormous lion with the caption that said, *"Every morning in Africa, a gazelle wakes up. It knows it must run faster than the fastest lion, or it will be killed...every morning a lion wakes up. It knows it must outrun the slowest gazelle or it will starve to death. It doesn't matter whether you are a lion or a gazelle...when the sun comes up, you'd better be running."*

This motto was Andrew's personal mantra—one that he reminded me of every chance he got. So, I knew that Matt was my best bet on the occasion of requiring creative thinking on a Friday night.

Just as I had hoped, Matt was more than willing to drop everything to leap at the chance to help me with this one. He was already well established with a prominent Bay Street law firm and typically knocked off work at seven most nights when he wasn't embroiled in a trial. By this time, it was nine p.m., and he'd had only one martini, so he hopped a cab and was at my door in fifteen minutes.

"Thank god for this distraction! I was immersed in briefs— I've got papers all over the apartment. Let's have a look at this," he said, reaching for the pages I had printed off the internet and that were now scattered on the floor. "What research have you done already?"

I seriously doubted that there were papers all over *his* apartment since it was one of those apartments that belonged in a magazine spread. Eschewing tony Yorkville, the uptown enclave of the rich and upwardly mobile, he had chosen to buy his first condo on the waterfront with a view across to the islands and the horizon beyond. It was breathtaking and impeccable, just like its owner.

To add to the pages he had picked up off the floor, I handed him a sheaf of papers I had printed out from even more things I'd found on the Internet. I had material about Javanese sarongs, Malawian *chitenges*, East African *kangas* and South African *kikois*.

"I'm particularly fond of how they do it in South Africa," I said, hiccupping. "They usually use them as throws on furniture. I'm thinking they make better throws than dresses."

Matt snorted at me, looked disdainfully at the label on the nearly empty wine bottle on the floor beside the coffee table and handed me the bottle he had brought. "Open this bottle of wine and take off your clothes."

Music to the ears of most normal young women whose boyfriend hasn't been able to stay awake for more than an hour or two at a time since they started dating, this remark was not actually what it sounded like. I knew better. First, Matt always brought his own wine because he usually viewed my selections with a certain degree of skepticism that often devolved into downright disdain. This judgement was usually not misplaced. He knows a great deal more about wine than I do. Second, of course, he intended to have me try on that annoying piece of fabric all six ways, taking a dim view of my feeble attempts to

9

make the six ways of wearing it work over a sweatshirt and a pair of Lululemmon yoga pants.

So, I did as I was told, went to the kitchen for two clean glasses whose shape might be appropriate for this wine, deftly opened the wine and poured two glasses. I was nothing if not highly skilled at removing corks from wine bottles. I did, after all, have a lot of practice. He made a ceremony of sniffing and swishing while I simply sipped. I disrobed as much as necessary and took another sip.

"Well," I said, swooning, "even if the dress doesn't change my life, this wine probably will. Maybe that's how I can lead off the story."

Matt smiled graciously. He always loved it when someone appreciated his taste in wine or clothing. He picked up the dress and my cell phone. "Start tweeting," he said."

"Tweeting? Whatever for?"

"Oh, Jenn. That expensive toy you carry around is for more than its looks. I know you don't like Twitter or any other social media for that matter, but if you can drum up some feedback about sarongs, pareos and dress draping in general, you just might come up with a good angle."

Now, why hadn't I thought of that? Perhaps it was the wine dulling my brain synapses, but no matter—all would be well now. And so it was.

I tied it over one shoulder and felt like Grace Kelly. I tied it around my neck and then up under my crotch, creating billowing legs and felt like Yul Brenner as the King of Siam (Okay, it would probably have been better to feel like Anna, but it was the best I could do). I tied it under my armpits, making a strapless number and felt like Paris Hilton. Then I'm sure I channelled Miley Cyrus when I tied it tighter under my crotch, creating a short-short, strapless jumpsuit that she might have worn in the days before she embraced nudity. Changing gears, I draped it over one shoulder and felt like Michelle Obama. But I could not, as hard as I tried, find the sixth. We had to fudge that one, but in the end, I had a lifestyle article. Eleanor absolutely loved it, and I sent Matt

10

a bottle of wine recommended by Eleanor's dry cleaner, who delivered her cleaning every Friday morning. Who knew that drycleaners knew that much about wine? I guess it comes in handy when trying to figure out how to remove wine stains from all those Armani suits. And thus, I was elevated to the grand position of assistant lifestyle editor.

I actually began to see that I could learn a great deal from Eleanor. Grudgingly, I had to admit that she was the consummate professional, even if she did get a bit carried away from time to time. She walked the talk. And that was never clearer to me than the time we ran a piece on Birkenstocks.

That one started with a media kit that a PR company sent to Eleanor containing a pair of patent leather, cherry red 'birkis' and a link to a YouTube video of a bra-less woman putting a pair of old, dirty, mouldy Birkenstock sandals into a compost bin. This whole situation seemed just wrong on so many levels.

First, the idea of Eleanor or any of the rest of us wearing Birkenstocks was laughable. This was before fashion designers all over the world started showing these footwear monstrosities with everything from swimsuits to business suits and even the odd evening gown. And it has to be said that this ghastly trend never really worked off the runway in real life anyway. In addition to the nature of the style in general, the thought of taking fashion or life advice from a woman over the age of 12 who needs to be introduced to the concept of a bra was appalling. Finally, I didn't ever want to see someone with her hands in a compost bin. It's not that I'm anti-composting – I'm as environmentally concerned as the next person. In fact, my father was one of the first in our town to have a compost bin in the backyard. It's just the idea of digging out the composting sandals after a couple of months and then feeling the slime and commenting on the bacteria that were now under your fingernails seemed so far removed from what we had been doing at *Vivacity*. Who knew that Eleanor was a closet environmentalist? Even she didn't know that you could compost sandals, and when she discovered that Birkenstocks were now available in a wide variety of cool colours and finishes, she decreed that they had become our new shoe of choice, and everyone in the office was to begin wearing them immediately.

The article was to be titled "Change your shoes, change your life." I was to write a draft, and then Eleanor would complete the piece herself. We were to do empirical research, Eleanor said, for the first three weeks of the sandal-wearing experiment. And everyone on staff was to be part of the data gathering. Did I mention that all of this happened several years before the appalling fashion tragedy that found designers of all stripes pairing these hideous monstrosities with everything from career-style dresses to ball gowns? I know I did – but it does bear repeating. Just thinking about it now gives me shivers. Blecch!

Under some duress, I put on my hibiscus pink gizeh's (don't ask), paired them with white linen pants and a short, fitted black jacket, and I was off and running. They were comfortable in a bizarre kind of way, but I couldn't shake the feeling that I looked a bit like a hippie wannabe who had lost her way when taking a wrong turn on the road to eco-consciousness.

If I thought I felt uncomfortable, I had nothing on the girls in reception and human resources who, as far as I could tell, would wear stilettos to run a marathon. Their pain was at least as physical as it was psychological. Although they were mortified at the image they thought they were projecting to their unsuspecting public—I know this because they moaned to anyone who would listen, anyone that is except Eleanor—they were actually in pain because years of stiletto-wearing meant that they all had Achilles tendons about the same puny length as everyone thinks your average ballerina *en pointe* has. They groaned non-stop, surreptitiously donning their stilettos before leaving the office lest anyone should see them in their sensible footwear.

No one was sure how long this little jag would last until one day, about three weeks into the new lifestyle, two of the interns decided to embrace it more fully. They did this by arriving at the office one morning sporting dung-coloured hemp pants replete with drawstrings at the waist. That might have gone unnoticed by Eleanor, but it turned out to be the same day that one of our two male 'creatives' decided to sport argyle socks with his sandals. I think he did it on purpose. Anyway, that was the beginning of the end. Literally.

Avoiding a Fate Worse than Death: Or Why It's Better to be a Bag Lady Than Move Home to Your Parents' Basement

E leanor would have told me that the title was too long. She would have looked at me over the top of her sparkly glasses and said, "But it does have possibilities, Sweetie." She would have said that—I just know it. But she probably will never get a chance since things began to fall apart shortly after the Birkenstock debacle.

I remember the exact moment when I came to the crashing realization that life as I had known it had changed. Three months after the "Birki" incident, I was sitting in my parents' basement in a room that my father had intended to make into a music room. He hadn't bargained on boomerang kids. I was wondering if Mom and Dad weren't upstairs this very moment saying, "We should have moved to that waterfront condo," thus avoiding the inevitability of knowing what you had to do when your daughter calls home from the big city saying, "I lost my job in this damn double-dip recession, and there aren't any around here. And I'm running out of money."

What's a parent to do? Evidently, not precisely what a twenty-seven-year-old daughter who hasn't lived in her small hometown, never mind with her parents, for more years than she was then able to count might have hoped. They opened their arms and home to me, although my old room was now inhabited by my younger sister Emma—their mid-life baby—who was just finishing high school. I had been hoping for an infusion of cash, but in my heart, I knew that this would not have been the way Dad would handle my crisis—I should have anticipated this reaction. Instead of cash, he offered me a job. But I'm getting ahead of myself yet again.

No one saw it coming—at least no one except Matt. A wise investor since high school, it seemed, Matt kept an ear to the ground—or at least an eye to the ticker tape constantly running across the bottom of his computer screen and his Blackberry when he wasn't busy being first assistant defence attorney in a courtroom. When the stock market started to tank the first time, he moved his money around to keep it safe. Then he began asking me how that freelance sideline was going. I had always intended to do a bit of writing on the side to build a freelance résumé for the future. I dreamed of a career as a 'real' writer who woke up at dawn, wrote for a few hours, strolled to a café and wrote some more, met with her agent and basked in the adulation of her adoring fans who waited with bated breath for her next novel. Just thinking about it now makes me kind of tingly with excitement. But between what was now three years (had I really been there for three years?) of office politics at *Vivacity*, researching peculiar lifestyle pieces, shopping for the fabulous wardrobe I hadn't been able to afford all those years in university, and dating Andrew when he could pry himself away from his office, I had just never gotten around to it. I still had not published a single freelance piece on any topic. Oh, I had scads of journals stuffed to overflowing with ideas, but nothing seemed to have gelled. Or maybe I was just too busy shopping, going to trendy 'hot' yoga and meeting friends for cocktails to get on with it.

One Thursday evening, after Matt and I had finished a pizza in my living room, he asked me again for about the third time in as many weeks.

"Okay," I said, putting down my near-empty wine glass on my new glass-topped coffee table, then delicately wiping tomato sauce from my chin with a monogrammed pink linen napkin. I had been madly buying homewares and tchotchkes in recent months.

"What precisely is on your mind? You know I haven't really done anything about it. I'm starting to feel guilty, and I don't even know why. So, why the sudden interest in my non-existent freelance career?"

"Jenn, you know I want the best for my best friend."

"I know that, Matt. What's your point?"

"You've never been that interested in anything to do with the economy in general, so you probably don't realize that things are tanking."

I smiled at him for his concern. "Matt, I do read the online news feeds, but you know that you don't have to worry about me. I don't have any money in the stock market – unlike you. I know that investors are nervous, and that means you, doesn't it?"

"To tell you the truth, I'm not really worried about my own investments," he said. "I have a very diversified portfolio…"

I must have looked puzzled. I could feel an economics lesson coming on, and my eyes started to glaze over. I held my hand up. "Stop! I know what a portfolio is; I just don't see why any of this has any effect on my freelance career aspirations."

Matt sighed and poured the rest of the wine. "Have you seen Andrew this week?"

A bit of a non sequitur, I thought, shaking my head. "We've been texting, but he's been working long hours."

"Do you have any idea why he's been working so much?"

I shrugged, secretly hoping that this line of questioning wasn't going to lead me to regret that I had never followed up on precisely what Andrew *did* in all those hours he couldn't spend with me. "He works so much that he doesn't like to talk about it when he's out of the office. I guess I might have stopped paying attention."

"I don't know if it's my place to say anything, but you know that two of my friends who I see at the gym work at Global Atlantic, too." Matt took a long sip of his wine before continuing. "They're in trouble."

16

Global Atlantic was the huge investment bank to which Andrew dedicated almost every waking moment of his life. It couldn't possibly be in any kind of trouble. They were huge. You know, too big to fail? Anyway, they'd been in business for years. They were multi-national, whatever that meant. "What kind of trouble?" I said.

"The financial kind."

I didn't know quite what to say. I was concerned for Andrew and, frankly, a bit hurt that he hadn't confided in me, but I still didn't get the connection between his bank's difficulties and my non-existent freelance writing career.

"Do you know where Eleanor got her money to start *Vivacity* eight years ago?"

I had never really thought about it. I only knew that she had been in business for several years before I joined her and that she owned the magazine, or at least I had always thought she did. I also thought that since we were all paid more than the industry average, she must be doing very well—financially speaking. It had never occurred to me that she owed anyone money because it wasn't part of my daily reality.

"Are we playing twenty questions? What are you trying to tell me?"

"I'm trying to tell you that the scuttlebutt around the gym is that Global Atlantic is about to call in its major loans to avoid bankruptcy. That means that places like *Vivacity* are very likely to go under. In case you didn't know, they own a good chunk of the magazine – silent partners, it seems."

I could hardly take in what Matt was saying. It couldn't be true. There was always gossip on Bay Street. And I was so happy there; things like this just didn't happen to me. Surely, he must be mistaken. I was trying to make sense of this when the phone rang. I looked at the caller ID and saw Andrew's home number flashing. That was odd; I thought he was still at the office. I glanced at my watch and saw that it was 7:45. Glancing toward Matt, who nodded, I picked it up.

"Jenn, I need to talk to you."

"Hey. What's up?"

He seemed excited in a happy kind of way, but I couldn't really get a sense of what was going on. "Can I come over? I need to talk to you."

"Sure. Matt's here." Matt started shaking his head and waving at me. He mouthed, *I'm leaving.* *See you on Sunday.* I nodded and blew him a kiss as he gathered his things and beat a hasty retreat.

Twenty minutes later, I opened my apartment door to find Andrew standing there holding a large bouquet of flowers. His eyes were wide and shiny, and his cheeks red, as if he might have just walked ten blocks. That could not possibly have been true, though. Andrew's mantra was *why walk when there are cabs*?

"Here," he said, thrusting the armload of flowers toward me. Then he took a bottle of what looked to be *Veuve Clicquot* champagne out from behind his back and held it out. "We're celebrating."

Wow, *Veuve*, my very favourite champagne, is $60 or $70 a bottle. This sounded good. Obviously, Matt's gym intelligence had been so wrong.

Andrew came in and made his way immediately to the kitchen for champagne flutes. I loved my champagne flutes – they were the kind where the champagne even filled the stems. I knew that they were all wrong (Matt had told me so on several occasions), that they warmed up the bubbles too much when you held the stem, but they looked divine.

Andrew came back with the flutes refusing to say anything until he had (expertly) opened the champagne and poured two glasses. We were seated on my new faux-suede, cream-coloured sofa.

"Here's to the future," he said, his eyes shining even brighter. I wondered at that moment if he might not already be drunk. As if reading my thoughts, he said, "I got a bit of a head start on you, so drink up." He practically chugged this exquisite elixir. I so rarely had a chance to savour a glass of *Veuve* that I had no intention of chugging.

I was starting to pick up on the excitement, too. We'd been dating for a while now. We got along wonderfully – when we were actually together, and texting was a great way to connect when we couldn't. Was he possibly going to...? Oh, god, I thought suddenly. He's going to do it. He's going to ask me to marry him. To my great surprise, my stomach started to roil, and I wondered if there was any way to get him to stop. I had considered what life might be like if we moved in together – but even that was not resonating with me at that moment. We hadn't been dating nearly long enough; I could hear my mother saying it over and over in my head.

"I have the most wonderful news." He unclipped his Blackberry from his belt, clicked a button and turned it around so I could see it.

I squinted until I could make out that it was an airline ticket. There were two names on it – mine was one.

"We're going to see the world," he said as if he had just won the lottery.

He had booked two tickets to Paris. Paris, I thought, the most romantic city in the world—at least, that's what everyone had said. I had never been there—although, as a little girl, I used to cut out magazine pictures of the Eiffel Tower and Parisian cafes. I thought that French women were the most stylish in the world, and when I started working for *Vivacity*, I realized that I wasn't the only one. My mind started doing its monkey-mind thing again, jumbling all my thoughts together at once. It was kind of thrilling to think about going to Paris. So, I looked at the ticket again to squint at the return date. There wasn't one.

"Wow, Andrew. You were listening when I told you I was taking a vacation in April." I hugged him, almost spilling my champagne because I was so excited that a proposal wasn't forthcoming. I quickly licked the glass. The one-way aspect of the tickets hadn't registered in my brain. Yet.

"No, no," he said, laughing. "You don't get it. They're for Sunday night."

19

"Sunday...? But..." My mind was ticking off the days. Today was Thursday. Sunday was three days away. Was he insane?

"We're going to see the world," he repeated. "Not just Paris; the world. That's just the start."

I sat back and tried to stop my thoughts from whirling so wildly. I put my champagne flute on the table and tried to grab hold of a coherent thought. The first one that I could get a hold of was, "But I have to work on Monday. My vacation doesn't start until..."

"No, you don't have to work on Monday. No one *has* to work on Monday," he said

Yes, I do, I thought.

"You're going to quit and come around the world with me. You know that you've always wanted to travel. Well, here's our chance. And you can make notes for that novel you want to write."

My head felt like it was going to explode. I picked up his Blackberry from where he had laid it on the coffee table and looked at it again. He reached for it and started scrolling.

"I did some research," he was saying, his fingers now racing across the miniature keypad.

I heard him, but his voice seemed very far away. *Could I do this?* I wondered. The little girl inside me was intrigued.

"This guy and his girlfriend did the same thing three months ago, and he's been keeping a blog ever since. Here, look at this." He put the tiny screen about six inches from my face. "We'll follow their route."

I took it from him and peered at the tiny screen. I started reading. The guy—Frank was his name if you can believe these blogs—sounded like a dork. And the picture in this blog post showed Frank and his girlfriend, Tina, backpacks bulging, standing proudly in front of a hostel with a sign that read, "Gothenburg Youth Hostel" in English below something in an uninterpretable language. "Where's Gothenburg?"

"Sweden," he said. "Isn't it exciting?"

I finally got a hold of myself, quickly placing the Blackberry back on the coffee table as if it had suddenly become red hot. "Wow, this is very sudden." I looked at him closely. "And very unlike you, I must say. Where did this idea come from so suddenly?"

Andrew picked up the bottle and took a swig. I was horrified—you just don't do that with *Veuve*. But I didn't say anything. Then he swigged again.

"Simple, really. It was right after I got to my desk this morning and saw the pink slip. Or maybe it was while the sheriff's assistants were rifling through my computer files. Or just maybe while two others were escorting me out of the building with my pitiful box of office paraphernalia." He stood up. "Anyway, I got some severance."

I didn't know what to say. He walked over to the window, gazing out silently for a moment. Things seemed to have begun moving in slow motion. He turned around. He had a kind of Mona Lisa-like smile tugging at the corners of his lips.

"You know, Jenn, I haven't felt this free since my first week in university when I knew that I didn't have to face my father's constant questioning every time I arrived home after curfew."

Then, out of the blue, it hit me. I didn't want to go around the world. More precisely, I didn't want to go around the world with Andrew. How could I say this to him? Especially when he'd just lost his job – and so humiliatingly.

"I don't want to go around the world with you," I blurted. There it was. I bit my lip and shut up.

To put it mildly, Andrew didn't take it well. First, he cajoled, and then he pouted. Then he ranted and raved for the next half hour or so, trying to convince me that this was 'our time.' I didn't hear any of his protestations. I knew that it was 'his time.' When he was through with his tirade, we sat side by side on the sofa, silently collecting our thoughts. I felt very odd. I could not think of a single thing to say to this man as our relationship sunk into the quicksand. I could almost hear the final sucking. Decisively, he stood up and headed toward the door.

He kissed me on the cheek and bid me a 'nice life.' He would be on that plane to Paris, and maybe he'd start a blog, he said as he was opening the apartment door. I almost suggested that he call it "Around the World Without a Date." But I didn't. For once, I put my mind in gear before my mouth and stifled the blurt.

Later, lying in bed, I texted Matt. *"You were right about Global. Andrew jobless. Left for Paris. Talk soon, J. "*

I was surprised when my little dinger went off—I had a text message. *"Everything OK? M."*

I had expected that Matt would be out on the town at this hour. *"I think so, call u later."* Yes, I know. The email talk is so high school, but it was our way.

Surprisingly, I slept the sleep of the dead that night and every night for the next two weeks. Two weeks to the day later, I was lying wide awake in my bed at three a.m., going over the events of the day and recalling Andrew's knee-jerk reaction to his lay-off (I'd had one text message with a selfie from him from the top of the Eiffel Tower). I don't know how long I was awake, but I was just dozing when my cell phone pinged.

Eleanor had texted all the staff, time-stamped four a.m. that morning.

"I hope you all know how much you mean to this magazine. It is because of your hard work, determination and belief with a passion for our mission at Vivacity Magazine that we have continued to surprise and please our loyal readers every month. Please join me in the board room at 11 am."

So that morning, we had ambled off to the boardroom at 11 a.m. as invited. Eleanor was not there yet. She always liked to make an entrance, waiting until the last of us had arrived before sweeping dramatically into each meeting and woe betide any straggler. If the straggler in question had worked there long enough, he or she knew enough to wait outside the door until noticed through the glass and invited in. No one was allowed to make an entrance as such after Eleanor. This day was no different. We were all at our seats around the large table when she swept in, looking as if she had not slept at all the night before. I could tell by the slight yet noticeable intake of collected breath that I was not alone in my astonishment at seeing our illustrious leader looking anything but on top of the world. Well, things just went downhill from there.

The bottom line: the magazine was taking a 'hiatus.' Presumably, this was code for having gone bankrupt, unable to meet financial obligations—including the next payroll.

All of Matt's questions about my freelance career over the past few months rushed back and caught me in the throat. I would not cry. I would not cry. Oh hell, I would – just not here in front of everyone, or anyone for that matter. I waited two days, then called my parents to tell them the bad news about their daughter.

Clumsily, I relayed the story of the meeting, Matt's predictions, and the dire job situation in Toronto's magazine industry. Mom and Dad both listened patiently at the other end of the line, where they were comfortably snuggled into their beautiful oceanside house. Dad spoke first.

"So," he said to me, "So, dear daughter, what's plan B?"

Your Ultimate Guide to 'Boomeranging': Or How to Return to the Nest and Keep Your Dignity

I'm here to tell you that I really don't think it can be done. There is no way to move back home with your parents and keep your dignity. Or at least that's how I felt the moment I walked back into my childhood home, knowing that I didn't have a place of my own to return to when the weekend was over. I had read about people (usually men) who had done this and came to love that their mothers welcomed them with open arms, cooking and cleaning for them – but my mother was not a bit like that. So I knew that morphing back into a teenager would be out of the question, and I was fairly sure that I didn't want to be a teenager again anyway.

I had actually written an article about the boomerang generation two years earlier. Eleanor had loved it. Did you know that more than 40% of young adults between twenty and twenty-nine years of age live at home with their parents? And did you know that in the 1980s, only 27% did? Lord how much more difficult it must be to be a young adult today! However, when I look back now on the research I had done and the way the article turned out in the end, I realized with a jolt that I had written the article from the same point of view as everyone else who had been writing about the phenomenon (pack journalism, anyone?). As the article took shape, it had turned into a piece that was sympathetic to the parents. You know the details: it's hard on parents financially and emotionally when they're ready for the

24

empty nest; you need to set the ground rules, charge rent, yadda, yadda, yadda. Despite my tender age and what should have been a well-honed ability to empathize with the 'boomerangers' themselves, I just didn't see it from their point of view. No doubt it was because I thought that there must be something wrong with them. Surely, they must be lazy freeloaders. After all, I and everyone I knew had a great job, an apartment and a healthy respect for the distance we had created—both physically and emotionally—from our parents. There's nothing like a dose of reality to help you see things more clearly.

Moving out of my apartment was the hardest thing I had ever done. I kept it for a full two months after that fateful day in the board room, thinking that I would surely find a job soon, but there just didn't seem to be any jobs. I pounded the pavement with everyone else in the city until my nest egg ran out. I couldn't even get a job at Starbucks. The manager eyed me suspiciously all through the interview and kept asking me about my Master's degree and how much money I had made in my previous job. When I told him, he said, "You made more money than I did last year." I knew in that moment that I was not destined to be a barista, even temporarily.

I came very close to berating myself for all of those expensive clothes that now hung in my closet as pitiful reminders that I had nowhere to wear them. There were my cherished Jimmy Choos that I thought of as a kind of marker for my financial success and being able to look after myself, winking at me as if to say, "Joke's on you, honey." I was actually beginning to resent my clothes – after all, if I had been more prudent with my money, I would have been able to hold out longer. That great job was just around the next corner. I could almost taste it. But after watching three of my acquaintances give up and move home, I knew that I might not be far behind.

So, I left the big smoke behind, pulling my car onto the Trans-Canada Highway heading east. After the two-day marathon drive to the East Coast, I found myself in the awkward position of having to ring the bell at the front door of my parents' rambling seaside home since I no longer had a key. God love my mother – she had taken an afternoon off from her watercolour painting class—she was the teacher, not the student—to be sure someone could let me in. She smiled at me and hugged me. I love my mother, but I knew that she would not be all happiness and light about this turn of events. She and my father were at that very moment looking forward to my younger sister Emma leaving for university in the fall. Emma had been an unexpected baby when my mother was forty-two, and my father was fifty. That was eighteen (long) years ago. They were more than ready to be empty-nesters. *But,* I thought, *Dad had offered.*

After I had settled into my makeshift room in the basement with its ceiling-level windows and the hum of the furnace in my head all night long, I began to look closely around my old hometown. Cork Harbour, home to 2500 full-time residents, was named after a little place on the south coast of Ireland, which is where the town fathers (and mothers, one can only presume) had hailed from. It was one of those peculiar kinds of places that ballooned to over 6000 residents in the summers, supplemented with a hearty share of tourists. I had not lived there full-time since I left for university, so I hadn't really noticed the number of new 'inns' and B & B's that had sprung up like crocuses in the spring. They were everywhere. It had always been a sleepy kind of place where the traffic in the summer made you yearn for November to come—that's when you could be assured that the tourists would be gone. Then, the only movement on the water would be caused by the Canada geese and the lobster boats. The weather was hideous in the winter—cold, damp, windy. No self-respecting tourist would be caught dead in our neck of the woods at that time of year, and most of the time, we liked it that way.

My father's business, however, thrived on the summer people and, in recent years, had become something of an online shopping destination. I wondered how the recession would affect the gourmet grocery business. I had asked him once after Matt had brought up the recession for the umpteenth time.

"Jenn, it's like this: in a recession, people might not be able to buy all of those big-ticket, luxury items that they could when times were better."

I could just feel his eyes straying to the $650 suede boots I happened to be wearing at the time.

"But," he continued, "a $10 jar of gourmet mustard—well, that's the kind of luxury everyone wants—and can afford."

My first night back at the family dinner table had been surreal. I no longer had a role that I understood or could play with ease. *This is only temporary*, I told myself, but regardless of the transient nature of my planned reduction in life stature, I knew I'd have to make an effort to make it work.

In any case, it did appear that Dad was right in his assessment of the recession-weary consumer. He had built his gourmet grocery empire of sorts in this little seaside town. But don't be misled: Dad wasn't any small-town red-neck who drove around in a pick-up truck with his baseball cap shading his eyes. He had a big-time MBA and twenty years of stress-inducing experience as a high-powered marketing executive when, 15 years earlier, Mom had convinced him that they should move back to their hometown where they had met, fallen in love, married and moved away to university together, he to study commerce and Mom to study fine arts. They had been the original Yuppie—very urban and quite professional—until that day when they told me, their twelve-year-old daughter, that she would have to uproot herself from the city and move. I was less than ecstatic. But it was our move to Cork Harbour that led me to meet Faith, my then-BFF, and now the prospect of being able to see her again on a more regular basis since I was moving home (temporarily) was actually appealing to me.

That said, at this juncture, Dad's internet business was booming, so I sort of felt like I might be able to write his ad copy and take care of the blog he said he hadn't had time to launch on his website. Maybe I could introduce him to Twitter and use the skills that Matt had inculcated in me. It's true, I was (and to this day, am not) a big social media fan, but I figured that Dad's business just might benefit from it, and I could learn as I went. Maybe I could make this work and broaden my skills into the bargain so that when the recession eased, and jobs were plentiful, I could offer even more to an employer. On the long solitary drive home, though, I had spent hours thinking about my future. I had concluded that maybe this was a terrific opportunity in a different way. Perhaps I could actually start that novel I'd wanted to write ever since grad school. But I didn't tell anyone that.

As I mentioned, this move was also a chance for me to rekindle my friendship with Faith, who had returned to her hometown immediately after graduating from university with her nursing degree. She had gotten a job at the local hospital working in the delivery room and then met the new obstetrician in town. They had gotten married almost immediately, but unlike the women of yesteryear, she had yet to give birth, despite her husband's desire to procreate, a situation she had shared with me briefly. I hoped that she hadn't yet had to succumb to the fertility treatment merry-go-round. We had drifted apart as women tend to do when one of them is married, and the other isn't, but I figured that being in town would change that.

As I helped my mother clear the table that first evening, I looked around and considered how truly lucky I was. I'd try very hard to be the best boomerang kid two parents could ever have (since it was only temporary). That was before Dad presented me with 'the shirt' three days later.

"Try it on," Dad said as he handed me the plastic-wrapped package.

At first, I didn't know what it was and could not for the life of me imagine what there was in Cork Harbour that I would possibly want to wear. I should have known by looking at the smirk on my father's face.

I carefully removed the tape and plastic to uncover a hunting green golf shirt that was all too familiar to me. In fact, my father was standing in front of me, wearing an exact replica of the specimen I had in my hands. I opened it and held it up in front of me in all its green and cotton glory. It had a white-tipped collar that could be fetchingly lifted to frame one's face – I know because I had often told Dad that he should ensure that all of his employees did this—men and women alike. It would make it look so much cooler.

On the left breast was a tasteful black and gold logo – golden bananas with black lettering.

I remember when Dad had designed the logo and chosen *Savoureaux*, the French word for 'tasty,' as the name of his new grocery venture. I smiled as I recalled him letting a certain annoying teenager have an opinion on it. My smile froze, though, when I noticed the delicate embroidery on the right sleeve just above the band. It said "Jenn" in the same font as the pretty logo font on the front.

"Try it on," he said again, still smirking.

"Um, sure, Dad, but…" I wasn't sure how to react except to begin connecting the dots that were floating around my head. *No, wait a minute, those aren't dots*, I thought. *They're stars, and I think I'm getting a bit light-headed.*

"Everyone wears them," he said. "You know that. That hasn't changed."

"But, Dad, I'm going to be upstairs in the office. Do I really have to wear it?" I think he chortled.

"Well, we're all always prepared," he said.

"Prepared for what?" Certainly not an impromptu visit by the fashion police, I was thinking.

"To work on the floor," he said. "I think it'll go very nicely with those boots you had on at dinner the other night."

He was talking about another very expensive pair of boots— in this case, smooth calf-skin leather in a very fetching shade of chartreuse. My father and I had an interesting relationship through my teenage years. He truly seemed to know me better than anyone else—especially my mother. She just thought I was too focused. As her own life veered more toward meditation and finding her true place on the planet (in front of a group of watercolour students willing to pay extortionist prices for her classes), mine zoomed off in the direction of traffic and $5.00 lattes and expensive shoes. My father 'had my number' as the saying goes. He knew exactly the buttons to push, but he was able to do it in a way that usually ended up making me smile. Hmm…could I get a smile out of this? Oh, maybe it was a joke.

"Jenn, I'm actually delighted that you're going to be here for a while. I haven't had much of a chance to be a part of your education. I realize that you're not planning to stay forever, but while you're here, I think it would be a great opportunity for you to see the inner workings of a successful retail enterprise."

I must have looked either shocked or perhaps deflated—I can't tell what he thought. I only knew that I didn't know how to respond.

"Look, Jenn, I know that this is not the life you had planned for yourself. But it seems to me that the one thing I might be able to teach you is that life is what happens when you're busy making plans."

"Want to make god laugh? Tell her your plans," I said wryly. Dad looked a bit confused. "It's something Eleanor, my boss, used to say."

"Well, I think you did learn something from her. Come on, Jenn. It'll be fun. Father and daughter in business together – at least for a while. I know you're probably hoping to write that great novel while you're here. I won't work you too hard. But you do have to wear the shirt!"

He was smiling broadly now, and I have to admit that he did make it sound like something of an adventure. I just wondered how he knew about my secret plan to write that novel. Maybe it wasn't as secret as I thought.

"Will I still be able to work on your new marketing campaign?"

"And on our website and our Facebook page…" He stopped and looked at the incredulous look on my face. "…and on our Twitter account. In fact, you can take that one over. I'm so sick of tweeting."

Tweeting? My father just said 'tweeting'? Maybe I didn't know my father as well as I should have. How could I not have known that he had a Twitter account? Did he ever wonder why I didn't follow it? I thought he needed a blog on the company website. Evidently, he did—it was just the one thing that they hadn't gotten to yet. Later, when I checked his Twitter feed and saw his follower numbers, my eyes nearly bugged right out. I suppose with 32,000 followers on Twitter, he might not have noticed that I wasn't following! He sure did have a ready audience for a blog, though.

Later, alone in my basement room, after checking out Dad's clever Facebook page and reading some of his witty tweets, I tried on the shirt. The colour actually didn't look bad on me. I held my cell up in front of me and snapped a selfie, which I immediately sent to Matt with the caption, "Me…and my new life."

Half an hour later, my Skype dinged on my laptop. It was Matt.

"I had to see with my own eyes," he said. "What the heck is going on out there in lobster-ville? Have you fallen victim to some kind of sartorial malaise?"

I had taken off the shirt but held it up in front of the webcam so he could see it. When I told him about my new gig, he started to laugh. He chided me for a few minutes about the unworn clothes that were now going to hang untouched in my closet.

"Well, at least some of them are classics—they won't go out of style too quickly. Besides," he said, "I fully expect you to return. I actually miss you already! Please, just don't start a blog, though. The world does not need any more blog-to-memoir books!"

Well, ditch that idea, then, I thought. Yeah, I missed Matt too. I also missed my life. Well, I thought to myself later when I peered up and out the window—I could just see the moon way up there—I'm going to have to choose either to put my life on hold while I'm here or maybe I could have a life here for a while.

Is Facebook Ruining Your 'Real' Life?

Back in grad school, I had, of course, studied Oscar Wilde. I wrote papers about him. I took umbrage at the very idea that he had been persecuted and imprisoned in his life for his sexual preferences (Matt told me to lighten up about that). I even auditioned for a part in his play *The Importance of Being Earnest*—for which I was seriously unsuccessful, being such a poor actor. But I did go to the play and loved every minute of it. But the one thing that stayed with me all those years was a quote attributed to Wilde. I wrote it on a piece of paper and put it inside my copy of the playbill. I didn't even have the sense to write down its source, but I had memorized it. "One's real life is often the life that one does not lead." And it was that quote that came to mind as I sat in front of the computer in the office up above Dad's flagship grocery store, thinking up clever tweets for his 'followers.' I was thinking about real lives and how cyberspace has changed all that.

I was as guilty as anyone else my age on the Facebook front. In fact, there's a study (no kidding—there really *is* a study) of why people use Facebook. The researchers found that we use it for two main reasons: because we need to belong and for what they called 'self-representation.' In my opinion, as a Facebook user, most of it is a specific form of self-representation: self-promotion! Personally, I used it to connect with far-flung (and sadly even close-flung) friends. I used it to peer at the photos of my friends' fabulous vacations. I used it to brag about my own accomplishments. I used it to lurk around my friends' friend lists.

All in all, it was a kind of ego-fluffing device that we couldn't get enough of. That said, now that I was back in Cork Harbour (temporarily), I realized what a great tool it could be: I could use it to keep connected (my need for belonging, but one has to ask, belonging to what precisely?), but I could also be assured that I could pick up my friendship with Faith just where we had left it off at the end of high school. You see, she had been one of the first people to 'friend' me on Facebook, and I felt like we were still a part of each other's lives. She had told me all about James, the love of her life, through personal messages on Facebook, and then I had looked at the photos that she often posted of them together, although I noticed that there were fewer and fewer. Anyway, because of all this Facebook interaction, I felt as if I already knew him. I had come home to attend her wedding, and to tell you the truth, this obstetrician (James) didn't quite live up to his advance press. His photos online were exceptionally flattering—and of course, photos could not be held accountable for not doing justice to his odd sense of humour—but I digress.

Sometime after the wedding, when I posted some of my own photos I'd taken that day in an online album for her, Faith was ecstatic. Faith had given me the thumbs-up for my writing accomplishments over the years and had faithfully read *Vivacity* every month. I clicked 'like' on all her pictures of hikes and lobster dinners and cruises to the Caribbean. Although we had rarely been able to connect in person, on the few occasions when I visited my parents, we were still BFFs, thanks to the wonders of cyberspace connecting. So, it was natural for me to send her a Facebook message to tell her the great news that I was now home.

I had expected an immediate response—or at least a response within twenty-four hours. However, the next day, I was still waiting. When I complained about this turn of events to Matt during one of our many texting sessions, his response was, "What did you expect? You never bother to see her when you're actually home. Why should she rush to see you now that you're without friends? BTW when are you coming back? The city is a bit drearier without you."

I smiled at this and messaged him as follows: "But we've been such good FB friends."

"A FB friend is not a real friend."

Here it was again; there was the notion of a real life versus—what? A made-up life? A cyber-life? I was beginning to realize that perhaps they were the same thing. Just then, I got a message. It was from Andrew, of all people! He was inviting me to subscribe to his blog.

Against my better judgment, I surfed over to his blog (which was not titled 'around the world without a date' as it turned out). But it *was* titled…

AROUND THE WORLD WITHOUT A SUIT

Are you kidding? I thought, snorting in a most unladylike fashion. And what was that about being able to get used to living in hostels? Andrew had told me on more than one occasion that since he had gotten his job as a stockbroker, he never intended to sleep in another bed with sheets whose thread count was under 600. I could not even imagine what kind of hostel had that kind of accommodation! Further, against my better judgment—I was beginning to wonder if I had any good judgment left—I clicked on that little orange spot in the corner to subscribe to his blog and wondered how long it would be before he cracked. It was too good to pass up!

Then, finally, I got a message from Faith. She would love to get together. She told me to call. So, I did.

If I could find one word to describe how I felt when I knocked on Faith's door, and she answered the door with a full face of make-up, in an outfit replete with two strands of pearls, with an enormous crystal chandelier twinkling behind her giving her a kind of angelic halo, that word would have to be single. Yes, I felt single. Single, as in not able to afford on my own the kind of luxury that waited behind the double doors of her McMansion – an oddity in Cork Harbour if ever there was one. She had been living in this house for over four years, and this was the first time I had ever darkened the doorstep. Yes, as she smiled and brushed a non-existent strand of hair from her face with her left hand, I felt very single. I had forgotten just how dazzling that chunk of yellow diamond in platinum that glinted from her ring finger was. I was momentarily blinded.

"Jenn!" she screeched as if she had not been expecting me when I was on her impressive doorstep at exactly the invited moment. "James, you'll just never guess who's here!" she said, turning her head slightly toward the interior.

Faith was now flinging her arms around me in a hug that would have impressed even a bear. I was momentarily puzzled on two counts. I was puzzled that James was home in the middle of the day (why she was home is a story I'll get to eventually), and I was completely bewildered about why she had to announce me in such a surprising way. Surely she had mentioned to her husband that she had invited me over?

James appeared from the depths of the house, a mug of coffee in hand, stethoscope slung casually around his neck. His quizzical expression turned quickly to one of—oh, I don't know, horror, perhaps—when he finally registered that it was me. This reaction didn't bode well.

James put his mug down on a strategically placed coaster on top of a marble-topped hall table and came over with his hand extended for me to shake. "He just popped home for lunch unexpectedly," she whispered in my ear while pretending to kiss me on the cheek. "He has a patient in labour, and things are going slowly."

"Jenn," he said, looking me up and down while pretending not to. "You look...well."

"Nice to see you too, James. I'm so glad you're keeping my very best friend well and happy."

Faith was beaming; James looked at me oddly.

"I'll just grab my coat," he said. "I'm sure you two have a lot to catch up on. Faith, darling, I'll see you at 5:12." With that, he disappeared again into the depths of the enormous house, and I was left thinking, *5:12? Why not 'around 5'?* What kind of person can tell the exact minute that he'll be home anyway? Especially one who delivers babies for a living.

Before I could ask the question, Faith led me into the living room.

"He wasn't supposed to be here," she was saying as she glanced out the window, waiting a moment to see James's car start to roll out of the driveway. She then kicked off her black-toed cream-coloured Chanel flats and plopped onto the enormous white sofa with its vast collection of carefully curated cushions.

I had seen a spread like that once before when we did a piece in *Vivacity* about how home décor mimics fashion and becomes your way of relating to the world. I suddenly began to see Faith's living room as a series of magazine photographs: carefully arranged groupings of black and white photographs on one wall, a grouping of watercolours on another; a vignette of marble-topped hall table with its Frank Lloyd Wright-inspired (or maybe original?) lamp on top, a pile of three leather-bound books and an amber vase on top; a fireplace flanked by two chairs that appeared to be right out of the latest issue of *Architectural Digest*. There wasn't a single sign of the intrusion of real life.

"Wow," I said to her when I finally had a chance to gather my thoughts. "This is an incredible room, Faith."

"Oh, this one," she said, looking around. "It's kind of a joke, isn't it? I mean, does it even look as if anyone actually lives here?"

God, Faith always could read my thoughts. I'd have to be more vigilant about the musings of my over-excitable cranium.

"Do you ever use it?" I said, looking around to take in all the perfection.

"With this white sofa? Too dangerous," she said, laughing.

I had written an article a few months before *Vivacity*'s demise about the new lifestyle gurus who promoted the notion of imperfect perfection. As an English major, I never was able to get my head around that paradox, I'm afraid. It seemed that the idea of everything looking perfect was somewhat out of style – truth be told, it had never been in style for me. One of the psychologists I interviewed had been careful to point out that the veneer of perfection espoused by recent design trends tended to suggest psychological imbalances in the owners of these rooms.

I was almost speechless. "It's, um…"

"Perfect?" she said. Faith smiled. "I read that article you wrote, you know."

Busted. The ice was broken.

"Yup, it is, isn't it?" she said, laughing. "But before you start psycho-analyzing me, I have to tell you that it's James's sanctuary. I've lately adopted a sort of artistic approach to living, which doesn't suit him very well. He comes in here to hide from me, I think."

I was thinking about the ways that Faith's adult life and mine had gone their separate ways.

Faith had lived at home and commuted an hour each way to the closest university where she had studied for a nursing degree. James had come to town 'from away' as Cork Harbourites liked to say, to set up his obstetrical practice sometime during her four years of study. His family evidently had quite a bit of money that his father had made when he sold his business in the western oil patch, a life that James had no interest in. He did like to flaunt it a bit—a big house, a Mercedes and a BMW in the driveway, high-end vacations. Anyway, he and Faith had become an item when she returned to Cork Harbour to work in the case room—the delivery room—of Cork Harbour Community Hospital.

I had always thought that Cork Harbour was one lucky little town to have its own obstetrician, but I had gleaned enough information about James to know that he was a bit of a control freak, and if he had worked in a large city, he would have been constrained by the local medical school. Here, he was master of his domain, the head of Obstetrics and Gynecology, a grand title even if he was the only OB-GYN in town. Anyway, he and Faith had married within six months. Some time later—I wasn't sure precisely when—she had given up her full-time job to be… Well, I wasn't exactly sure what she was doing these days, to tell the truth, but I figured I was about to find out.

"Before we get comfortable," Faith said, going over to a large cabinet, "we need a bit of lubrication."

She pressed a button (yes, it's not just in movies; people really do have these things in their homes, at least my wealthy friend does), and the door slid around and to the side. The cabinet housed a dizzying array of liquors.

I looked at my watch—it was kind of a Pavlovian habit of mine. I was completely conditioned to knowing if it was late enough to rationalize a drink. I had started it when Matt and I would occasionally study together. I had been known to intone that it was noon somewhere in the world, usually Newfoundland, since it was the only place I knew about in the world where noon arrived half an hour earlier than in other places (or something like that). Anyway, it was almost 1:30, so we were okay.

"This," she said, taking two martini glasses from a dazzling display of crystal, fully lit and backed by mirrors, "is the reason James likes it in here so much."

My eyebrows must have risen noticeably.

Faith laughed. "No, don't get me wrong," she was saying, "James isn't really much of a drinker. He just likes the kind of Mad-Menesque feel of old-fashioned martini and champagne glasses." She picked up what looked like a '30s-inspired champagne coupe, the kind I usually salivated over, all the while listening to Matt tell me that the old coupes caused the champagne to lose its bubbles too quickly. But they were so glamorous, I remembered saying to him. He had been adamant: champagne is to be served in flutes. He did frown, however, at my flutes with the fill-up stems, as I may have mentioned.

Faith expertly and quickly mixed two martinis: gin, a splash of vodka and a splash of Lillet, shaken and served with three olives (everyone else used lemon peel), just like we used to like them back in the day. She brought mine over to me in the most intricate, cut crystal martini glass I had ever seen. We clinked softly and took a sip.

"So, tell me everything," she said as if she were starved for a good story.

Well, since it had been my stock in trade, I knew just how to make a story good, so I started.

I started from the beginning, and Faith hung on every word as I slightly embellished the bit about Andrew's dramatic entrance that fateful night and then the meeting where we all learned that we'd been given the pink slips.

"What did you do with all your Jimmy Choo's?"

With that question, I knew that all was right in the world once again. I smiled; Faith had been my style coach for so many years. It might seem natural to you that the one of us with the 'fabulous' job in the city with access to every manner of store available to the shopping woman might be the leader on this front, but Faith was nothing if not the most well-dressed, small-town girl I had ever met. She read every fashion magazine on the planet—even the ones in French. That's what motivated her to take an online French course and an online Spanish course when we were in high school. She wanted to be able to read *Vogue* (both from Paris and Spain) and *Marie-Claire*. She was now fluently trilingual, thanks both to those online courses and frequent trips to both France and Spain, and she was almost as much of a magazine junkie as I was—we were kind of co-dependent in those days. She was, however, a bit more discriminating in her selections than I was. She stuck to fashion magazines and *Vivacity*, but only the latter because I worked there. I, on the other hand, was a bit of a magazine whore collecting everything from *Elle* to *The New Yorker* to *The Economist* (that one was just to put on the coffee table to impress some of the men I was dating – turns out it was a stupid move anyway).

In any case, after mastering the languages, Faith trawled the online shopping sites, learning exactly where she could buy what she needed for any season. I never did understand her foray into nursing. I had electronically nagged her for years to either start a fashion blog or open a boutique in town. The tourists would love it, I used to tell her *ad nauseum*, and if she sold online as well, she'd make a killing or, at the very least, have fabulous clothes at cost. She always demurred. It seemed that James wasn't so enthralled with the idea, so she had put it aside, but I had always suspected that he had forbidden her to do it. That thought always brought out the rabid feminist in me.

After I finished my story and Faith had poured another round of martinis while glancing at her watch (a Cartier, I think) and murmuring something about not having to start dinner for an hour or two, I turned the conversation to her. She seemed a bit uptight whenever the topic turned to James and the life they were leading.

"So I guess you didn't tell James that I was coming over today."

Faith daintily sipped her martini like Doris Day might have done in the old movies. "Is that an observation or a question?"

"Faith, we've been friends for too long…"

"Well, it might have slipped my mind." She sipped her drink. "Okay, it's true. I didn't actually mention to him that you were coming over. I guess I might have also forgotten to tell him that you've moved back."

"Temporarily," I interjected.

She waved a hand dismissively. The martini was starting to take hold. "Whatever. Anyway, to tell you the truth, best friend to best friend, James isn't too fond of you."

I was (almost) speechless. I could actually feel my jaw drop ever so slightly. Who wouldn't like me? Of course, in case you haven't figured it out yet, the feeling was mutual.

Faith now took a big gulp and then set her glass down on the marble table—there were marble tables everywhere, it seemed—spilling just a tiny drop, which she quickly mopped up with a cushion. She hiccupped delicately. "It's like this, Jenn. James thinks you're a bad influence on me. Not that I really care." She hiccupped again. "In fact, not that I need influence to be bad," she said as an afterthought and almost inaudibly. She then sat back and waited for me to respond.

"A bad influence? He's only met me twice before in his entire life. He based his assessment of my character on two brief encounters in crowds? And besides, how could I have been a bad influence from such a distance?" I was thinking about their wedding and one other time where we had run into one another when I was home. It seemed we were never able to get together formally on those weekends.

"Oh, Jenn, it's not so much your character as your lifestyle."

"That really clears things up," I said rather unnecessarily sarcastically.

"I mean, I'm a… Oh, Jenn, I'm a doctor's wife."

"So you are. So what? And by the way, when did you stop working?"

"I work," she said, feigning a pout. "Believe me, I work even when I'm not working. I work in James's office two afternoons a week. You know, James actually has pretty old-fashioned ideas about wifedom and motherhood." She screwed up her face. "Is wifedom a word?"

"Motherhood? You don't have any children. Or have you been holding out on me?"

"James is keen. Me Not so much." She sipped her drink. "Anyway, there's a lot to being a doctor's wife, I guess."

I just sat there, sipping my drink, arms crossed over my chest, thinking about how I might be a bad influence on a wife and someday mother who happened to be a long-time friend who had shoes older than her relationship with James – the interloper.

"So," I said finally, "Do tell. What do you do the rest of the week when you're not at James's office?"

Faith had imbibed just enough liquor to loosen her tongue. It turned out that James the doctor had ideas that belonged on a 1960s sitcom—or maybe in *Mad Men* if he had a better wardrobe. He really had this idea that his doctor's wife would stay at home vacuuming in her pearls and pencil skirt. Faith had found it charming – for about a year. Then, she had begun to get restless. The internet, it turned out, had been her saviour—although it had resulted in her breaking her clothing budget. It seemed she was a bit of an online shopaholic.

"Once I thought that I should write an article for your magazine on the perils of online shopping, but James thought that it was a bad idea. He didn't want anyone to think he was stingy and wouldn't let his wife shop."

Let his wife shop? It occurred to me that there was more at stake here than a bit of over-budget spending, but I thought better of opening my mouth about it—yet.

"You know, Jenn, James isn't really so bad, it's just that...Well, it's..."

"It's what?"

"Have you ever watched anyone floss his teeth? I mean, really floss—and really look?"

I had to admit that I had never really watched someone floss. Now that I think about it, I don't think it was something that I'd like to do under any circumstances. I always felt that there was something private about it. It was not unlike how I felt about people who sat on the toilet with the bathroom door open, carrying on a conversation between grunts. It was just wrong. But I wondered what watching someone floss had to do with whatever it was that Faith wasn't telling me.

"Well, James is a bit of a health nut. He believes that flossing is at the heart of preventing inflammation—or something like that. Anyway, he walks around the house flossing and talking. But the worst of it is that between every tooth, he takes the piece of floss and examines it. I mean, he really looks at what he's just scraped off his tooth. It's disgusting. Do you think that it's a doctor thing?"

I thought that his professional bent might have made him more likely to be interested in things that happened in stirrups, but I had a deep belief that manners ought to trump those kinds of pursuits. Anyway, I didn't really know where this was going, except it occurred to me that, for all Faith's perfection in face, body and homestead, she was not a happy camper.

"You know...I do love James," she said again.

"So you keep saying." The liquor was starting to loosen up my own tongue now. I could feel myself on the verge of saying something sarcastic about James and his tendencies. I stopped short of reminding Faith that he'd shown up at their wedding 45 minutes late with the announcement that he had been needed in the delivery room. He couldn't give up control to the new midwife in town, even on his wedding day.

"Oh, Jenn, my life is just so predictable. We see the same people at the same cocktail parties, drinking the same drinks and having the same conversations week after week after week. I could just scream. And now that you've moved back to town—"

"Temporarily," I interupted her.

"Back to town, I don't have an exciting lifeline out there in urban land. You were the balance I needed, even if it was only vicariously."

I had no idea that Faith had felt this way. I always thought that she kind of took a dim view of my life, but that since we were such close friends, she was open-minded. I never thought that I was such an important part of her day-to-day life and, even more to the point, her connection with the outside world, so to speak.

She suddenly looked at her watch and jumped up as if conditioned. She picked up the glasses, went over to the wet bar, hastily rinsed them, dried them, and put them back on the shelf, which she then closed. Then she held her hand up in front of her mouth and sniffed her breath, or at least that's what it looked like from where I was sitting. "Oh, God," she said, "I smell like a distillery. Got to do something about that before James gets home."

It was time for me to leave. I didn't know what we would do next or how we'd deal with this admission of Faith's. I figured my best bet was to get another job and move back to Toronto. Even Matt was pining for me there, and the least I could do was give Faith her life back. But something told me that this wasn't the solution.

Friends with Money: Just Watch Those Relationships Change

I just love Woody Allen. All that angst. All of that nuttiness in those New York families. All those pithy lines. I guess that since my own life growing up was so different, I lived vicariously through his characters when I sat in those theatres through the years. I didn't live in a megalopolis, at least not such a big one; I didn't have nutty characters in my life; I had no angst—at least, I realize that as I look back. Pre-pubescent girls always think they have angst – I certainly didn't. Despite the world of difference between a Woody Allen character and me, I realize that Woody Allen also has a kind of approach to life that often resonates with me. I once read an interview where the writer quoted him as saying, "Money is better than poverty, if only for financial reasons." Ain't that the truth?

I was beginning to get the hang of what he meant. Sure, I had been a relative pauper in graduate school, but it's funny how quickly you get used to having a cash flow once it starts. When it came to an end, I didn't know how to adapt. For the first week after I returned home, I would walk around the house each day, looking at what was the same and what had changed. I had a lot of time to myself since Dad was busy from morning to night with the business, and Mom had her painting students in a studio she rented downtown—I use the word loosely since Cork Harbour was hardly big enough to have a downtown. Emma, of course, was in school, and Dad said I should have a few days to get my bearings before I started working with him. I suppose I should have been pounding out applications on my laptop, but I was paralyzed with indecision.

Should I have stayed in the city despite my growing insolvency? Should I have worked harder on my freelance career like Matt had nagged me to do? Should I be doing that now? Should I be sending out multiple query letters for magazine ideas? Okay, I was a bit short on ideas, but I was certain if I just sat down and thought about it, dozens of ideas would flood my brain. Should I just go to work for Dad and do the very best I could? Only this last one had any whiff of feasibility about it, so at the end of the week, I told Dad that I was ready.

On Monday morning, I was ensconced in the office over the store, looking at newsletter layouts and website designs. Oh, and I was wearing the green polo with a pair of designer jeans—and my Jimmy Choo Lennox pumps with their demure 1.3-inch heels in what I liked to call leopard patent. I thought that they would be the most sensible shoes to wear in a warehouse-cum-office space that had linoleum over concrete floors. I threw a white wrap around me and thought I looked rather fetching. Okay, I was only going to be making $10 an hour, but I could still look good. Dad had told me to set aside an hour a day for my job search, but other than that, I could expect to be fully engaged with *Savoreaux* and its marketing needs. After updating the web site, I was supposed to come up with a new tag line for the spring gourmet sauce promotion.

This kind of activity went on all week. I dutifully went to the office at 8:30 every morning and took a cup of gourmet blend Costa Rican coffee up the spiral staircase in the middle of the store—Dad let all of his employees freely imbibe the coffee because he was adamantly opposed to anyone drinking inferior coffee. God forbid that anyone should stop by Tim Horton's on the way to work and arrive with a disposable cup. Anyway, I think that was why they were all so perky. It was like a bottomless pot of caffeine. And so it went.

By Thursday, I was pretty sick of the green shirt. I was despairing of ever having enough ways to make it work stylistically when, all at once it hit me. Here was an idea for my first free-lance article—how to style a uniform. Now, all I had to do was find a magazine that was looking for writers with ideas about how to write about such trivial matters. Right on cue, I got a text message from Faith. She was inviting me out for dinner on Friday night. It would be just the two of us, and she wanted to try a new chichi restaurant that had just opened in town for the tourist trade. I was just about to jump at the opportunity when it occurred to me that I couldn't afford it. I. Could. Not. Afford. It. What kind of excuse could I make up? I could hardly tell her that I had to wash my hair. What would I tell a guy if I didn't want to go out with him? But I did want to go with Faith. What if I just told her the truth and asked if we could go someplace cheaper? So that's what I did. She texted back immediately.

"You twit. Of course, it's my treat. F."

Just this once, I thought to myself. *I'll let her pay just this once.* As I texted her back, I was interrupted by Dad's floor manager, Edward, who had made the trek up the winding stairs to ask me to come downstairs to help. I had been steeling myself for this. I was not what one might refer to as a hands-on kind of girl in that truest sense. In fact, the only time I really wanted my hands on fruits and vegetables was when raising said items to my mouth to take a bite. I wasn't much of a cook – the Julie/Julia's of the world notwithstanding. I read that book and found the food preparation scenes totally icky. I could not, however, say no to Edward (Dad had already made this point quite clear), so I dutifully followed him down the stairs, reflexively examining my manicure. I was still a cuticle girl from my days with Eleanor.

That day, I helped stack something called dragon fruit. *What kind of people eat something called dragon fruit*, I wondered? Again, I allowed a question that was quite happily making its home in my mind to make its unfortunate way to the tip of my tongue. Before I knew what was happening, I found myself voicing this particular question within earshot of Edward, who was something of a fruit fanatic, as it turns out.

"It does kind of look like a dragon's fire breath," I said, taking one of the items in question from a crate marked "Product of Mexico" and examining it more closely.

Edward was across the counter from me where he was helping one of the other girls—Ardyth, I think her name was—to place some kind of spiky things in artistic mounds. He stood up and looked at me with his hands on his scrawny hips. He just looked so vegetarian to me. I mean, I have yet to meet a fat vegetarian, although I'm told they do exist—at least where their vegetable of choice is the French fry. I have also yet to meet a vegetarian who actually looked healthy. He was a prize specimen, although I was only surmising about him being a vegetarian—slightly pale, thin, a bit of flakey skin on the exposed forearms that poked out beneath the ubiquitous green polo—although his logo was larger, presumably to indicate that he was in charge. Sometimes, if I squinted, though, I even thought he might be a bit attractive, but only if he'd just have a steak. He was scowling at me.

"Jenn," he said, obviously trying to contain himself no doubt because I was the boss's daughter, and he'd been saddled with me. "Jenn, we are a bit more respectful of fruits around here."

I started to snicker, thinking of the juiciest comeback. But this time, I held my tongue.

"Well, I guess you can't be expected to understand, given your background, but it's going to be my job to educate you."

Uh-oh, I thought. *I'm in trouble now.*

He picked up one of the red and green items and held it lovingly. "The dragon fruit, more precisely known as the pitaya, is native to Mexico and parts of Central and South America. These particular specimens are from Mexico and are what are referred to as red pitayas. You might consider taking one home this evening to try making a smoothie with the pulp, which you'll find will resemble thick poppy seed dressing when it's ready."

"They're actually kind of good."

I looked over at tiny red-headed Ardyth, who had spoken for the very first time since I'd arrived earlier in the week. I was thinking that I must make a point of befriending her. She was a bit mousy and seemed to be quite overwhelmed by my presence – no doubt because of my killer styling of the green shirt. Or perhaps it was because I am the boss's daughter?

I gently placed the dragon fruit that I was still holding onto the growing pile and thanked him for his lesson. All the time he was speaking, I was forming an idea in my head about an article I thought I might write about the new fruits and how they were representative of a particular lifestyle. I'd have to start taking notes. Who knew that a grocery store could inspire so many ideas?

It was hard work being on the grocery floor, I have to admit. I was much more cut out to be sitting in the office, trawling in front of the computer. But I did realize that if this was going to work out and get me back to where I needed to be, I'd have to do whatever it took.

On Friday night, I met Faith on Water Street in a bistro called *Le Crème*. She was waiting for me at a table by the window with candlelight dancing on her face. She may have been a small-town girl, but she was still a stunner with her long blonde hair swept up into a sort of *Mad Men-esque* French twist and her gorgeous turquoise wrap flung casually around her shoulders. James's proclivities for all things retro must have rubbed off on her, but somehow, it worked. She didn't see me at first. She had her chin resting on her hand and was gazing out at the water as it lapped on the rocks below. She looked a bit melancholy. I wondered what she was so deep in thought about.

The restaurant was on the ground floor of a new condo complex. (Who knew that there would ever be condos in Cork Harbour?) The condo building didn't resemble urban condo buildings in the slightest, though. It had the look of an overgrown waterfront warehouse with all the quaint touches that architects think appeal to condo dwellers. It had dormer windows on the topmost floors and balconies overlooking the water.

We ate fried calamari with curry dipping sauce, followed by halibut with orange and salsa verde washed down with a French

Viognier. Faith had been taking wine-tasting classes at, of all places, *Savoreux*. Evidently, my father had neglected to tell me that he brought in a sommelier once a month in the winter and weekly in the summer to conduct these classes in the back room that I had wondered about. Newly renovated since my last visit home, it had dark wood walls and exposed beams with a long table flanked by benches. There was also a wrought-iron chandelier of sorts that, now that I thought about it provided just the right ambience for a wine-tasting course. According to Faith, the viognier had a young, heady flavour that complemented the citrus of the chicken glaze. I was willing to take her at her word, but four glasses later, I thought she was a genius. I also noted, much to my surprise, that the menu proclaimed that all of the fresh produce and meat products were supplied by *Savoreaux*. Good for Dad!

We spent the evening talking and laughing about old times, assiduously avoiding my current financial and career crisis and her own situation as a 1960s housewife, apart from her murmuring something about James being very good about 'letting' her out for the evening. Was there a ball and chain I didn't know about? I decided to let it go and just enjoy my evening. When the server brought the bill at the end, I did have a moment of panic. Should I really be letting her pay? I was thinking this while she was telling me about the cruise James wanted her to book. The suite sounded wonderful; the butler sounded divine. I momentarily wondered why she didn't seem at all excited about it, but my seething jealousy – of the friendliest kind – just got in the way of pursuing that subject.

I messaged Matt later that evening, but he was obviously busy. When we did connect later in the weekend, he wanted to know everything about my still non-existent freelance career. At least I could tell him about those ideas that had come to me through the week. Now, if I could just start writing them down somewhere.

The following week started much the same as the one before. I went to work in the office; Edward inevitably called me downstairs each day for an hour to help with something or other. He then proceeded to tell me about yet another exotic fruit. The work may have been a pretext for him to simply school me in the finer points of exotic fruits and vegetables. It did occur to me that he might just have been doing this at Dad's behest. I'd have to remember to ask. On Tuesday, it was star fruit. After tasting that one, I decided that star fruit was just for garnish. On Thursday, the store was sampling avocadoes from Costa Rica that had shipped in with the week's supply of coffee beans that were still in their crates in the warehouse. I loved coffee and welcomed the opportunity to help with the shelving of that order. I could drink in the smell as I worked. Well, be careful what you wish for.

On Friday morning, my presence on the grocery floor was not so much requested as I was drawn of my own accord. I think it was that first blood-curdling scream that wafted up the spiral staircase that first got me out of my computer chair. By the third one, I could tell that it was Ardyth, and it sounded as if someone were trying to kill her. Had vegetarian-like Edward actually summoned up enough strength to strangle her? No, it couldn't be.

By the time I reached the bottom of the stairs, a group of employees and customers had formed a ring around the banana display. Ardyth was screaming and pointing.

"There," she said breathlessly, her arms wrapped tightly around herself when she wasn't letting one out to jab a finger in the direction of a half-empty crate of bananas. "I saw it there."

Ardyth did not look hurt, so I suddenly became curious when I noticed that Faith was in the store. She was standing beside Edward with one of our mini grocery carts in front of her, apparently engrossed in the scene. I made my way around the perimeter of the crowd to where I was beside Faith. As I did so, Edward moved away and into the fray. "What's going on?"

Faith looked at me, and I could actually tell she was checking out my outfit, green polo and all. Her nose started to twitch. I'd have to talk to her about that later.

"As far as I can tell, Ardyth saw a bug."

50

"Not just a bug," Ardyth screeched. "It's a spider. It's an enormous spider!"

By this time, my father had arrived on the scene, cell phone in hand. He was able to calm everyone down and assure them that occasionally, the fruit orders did, indeed, bring along stowaways and that they were more than capable of handling it. The crowd started to disperse. As Faith turned back to her cart, she seemed to have forgotten something.

"Oh, Jenn, I've been meaning to drop over to see you this week. I have a box of clothes for you. I think you might like them. They're not off this year's runways, but we're still about the same size. They'll fit. They're kind of lady-farmer kind of stuff: two quilted jackets, a couple of fleeces, you know, the kind of things that we wear in Cork Harbour in the winter. You probably don't have anything like that, and something new is always nice!" Then she actually winked at me.

I was having trouble processing this piece of information. Used clothes? Faith was giving me hand-me-downs? Before my good sense could kick in and tell me that anything Faith wore last year would be perfect this year, all I could think about was that I had sunk to a new low. Before I could respond and tell her that I had actually brought most of my own designer clothes with me (and that they were still in boxes and that I did, in fact, own winter clothes), she had made her way toward the cashier, and Dad was tapping me on the shoulder.

"Jenn, Ardyth is a little freaked out. Could you take her over to the coffee aisle? I was going to get you to do it later but now seems like a good time. The two of you could unpack those cartons. Do you see them? I just put them there. You can stack those bags of coffee beans on that new wall unit." He bent his head close to my ear so that only I could hear. "Jenn, keep an eye on Ardyth. You open all the boxes yourself, will you?"

I nodded, took Ardyth by the arm and led her over to the coffee, which put a fair distance between her and the alleged spider. She was actually shaking.

I talked her down with bits and pieces of small talk about Toronto, shopping at Holt Renfrew, designer clothes and men. She didn't say much, but I could tell that she was listening. That is until a great commotion started up again over by the bananas.

"There it is," shouted one of the customers. An older woman wearing a Tilley hat was gesticulating wildly. "Don't anyone move! And for god's sake, don't harm it! It might be a rare specimen."

A rare specimen? What was she—an entomologist? Edward was immediately upon her, shushing and trying to move her away. He was clearly trying to calm everything down– there's nothing worse than panic in the fruit aisle.

I was only mildly interested—I mean, how can you get that fired up about an insect? I turned to Ardyth, who seemed to be morbidly fascinated with the whole thing.

"I thought you were petrified of spiders," I said to her as she started to move toward the bananas.

"I really just need to see it," she said.

I could hardly hear her. I put another bag of coffee beans on the shelf, closed my eyes and breathed in deeply. I always found the smell of fresh coffee oddly calming. It's funny, isn't it? We drink coffee for that wake-up, and yet the smell is so soothing. I lifted another bag out and noticed that there was something stuck to it. *Good god*, I thought. *Not another damn bug! Does Costa Rica make money exporting their wildlife?* But it wasn't a bug. It was a piece of paper, and it seemed to be stuck to the bag. In fact, when I looked more closely, it wasn't just stuck randomly; it was taped.

I removed it carefully from the bag in an effort not to tear it – if the bag tore, it wouldn't be saleable. One thing I learned about the gourmet grocery customer is that she (or he) would never buy an item whose packaging was in any way compromised. It did not matter in the least if the interior was not touched. The packaging had to look pristine.

I got it off successfully and then unfolded it. I'm not sure what I expected to see, but I certainly did not expect it to have a handwritten note inside. The handwriting looked kind of masculine and a bit messy. I was momentarily reminded of my doctor's prescriptions for my birth control pills. I was always amazed that the pharmacist could even read them, let alone get the right dosage. But back to the note. I glanced over at the crowd that was clearly on the hunt for the offending spider, with Ardyth at the periphery, her hands behind her back. Then I spied one of the step stools that we used to put items on high shelves, sat down and started reading.

"To whoever finds this [the editor in me immediately noted the grammar—sounds formal, but unless I'm mistaken, not entirely correct]:

I am certain that you are a person of significant kindness [of course I am; how did you know?]. *When you read this note, please be aware that I am in need of assistance. The situation, however perplexing it might be, is not dire. Yet. I am most interested in your help should you be so kind as to follow up. If you feel that you cannot assist, I completely understand. Life is complicated. I remain your great admirer in any case, wherever in the world you might be. With respect, Juan Val Dez, Costa Rica."*

Juan Val Dez? What kind of a name is that? Then I remembered and started to giggle: the name of the fictitious coffee grower in those old TV ads. I turned the paper over as if there might be a clue as to the source of what was obviously some kind of a joke or scam. It was blank. I glanced over at the carton that had been sealed with a customs seal until we opened it this morning. The only thing I noted was the logo on the side of the carton – the same one that adorned every bag of coffee I had just stacked.

Café Exquisito it read. I was reminded of the email scams that all began with, "Dear kind sir or madam: I am in great need of your help to stash $20 million…blah, blah, blah."

Just at that moment, another commotion started up over by the bananas. Evidently, someone had caught the offending insect or whatever it was. Our entomology lady was holding it aloft in a plastic container that we used to dish up the gourmet takeaway salads. It was one of the large ones. I slid the note into my pocket and then went over to take a closer look.

"It's from the family *Theraphosidae*," she was saying to the rapt audience. "It is not an insect. It is an arachnid."

"Looks like a bug to me," one of the other shoppers said. "A very big bug."

It just looked kind of hairy to me, and then it dawned on me: it was a tarantula! Every B-horror movie I'd ever seen seemed to have tarantulas loose in the desert, but I had never seen one where the arachnids were loose in a grocery store. Maybe that would make a great movie.

"That's actually a tarantula!" I said, my hand flying to my mouth as if to protect it from wandering arachnids.

The woman in the Tilley hat holding the bottled spider looked at me in what appeared to be exasperation. It was the kind of withering look that you might give to a pea-brained person considerably below your level of intellectual capacity. That would be me in this case.

"My dear girl," she said with an expression that looked as if she were sucking a lemon, "That's what I said. The family *Theraphosidae*."

Well, I'd been told. I guess everyone—not just those who win big on *Jeopardy*—knew, and I was the odd man out. Oh well. I thought that my life had not really been diminished by failing to grasp that portion of my grade nine biology course. But it was a fascinating specimen – as long as she didn't let it out.

So much excitement could not be left behind without some kind of immortalization in cyberspace, so as soon as I got home, I posted a status report on my Facebook profile. After dinner, I had a message from Matt. "Call me tonight," it said.

I took a glass of excellent wine that Mom had received as a gift from one of her art students that day to my dungeon room and settled in to connect with those I'd left behind. I checked my email and then picked up my phone to call Matt. I reached into my pocket to check for tissues before throwing the pants in the laundry, and the piece of paper with the odd note came out instead. I was about to toss it in the wastebasket when I was suddenly seized by the idea that I shouldn't be so hasty in getting rid of it. Maybe it was some kind of existential message for me.

Cryptic, though it might have been, I was sure that if I thought about it in a couple of different ways, I'd get the message. Maybe it was supposed to be an idea for a magazine article. Or maybe it was the beginning of a plot for the greatest novel of the 21st century. Or perhaps it was telling me I should have gone with Andrew. Scratch that last one. I had been reading his blog, and the great adventure seemed to be wearing a bit thin.

The phone rang three times. I could picture Matt's perfect apartment with all of its contemporary loveliness just so. I could picture him taking his wine glass off the granite-topped breakfast bar and reaching for his Blackberry which he always left on the end table nearest the door when he came in. I could picture him plopping down on the white leather sofa, plumping up a gray velour pillow behind him to get comfortable for a long chat with his best friend. I pinned the note to the small corkboard I had installed over the tiny desk where I pretended to be a great writer and picked up the phone.

Holding the phone to my ear, I was contemplating the difference between Matt's surroundings and my new digs with their Murphy bed, bad television and tiny windows.

"When are you coming home?"

Matt had taken to never saying hello to me; instead, he greeted me with the same question each time. I suppose it was intended to keep the thought front and centre in my mind. It was working.

I then proceeded to tell him all about the spider incident. By the time I was finished, he was laughing so hard that I worried he might spill his wine (which was most likely red) on that beautiful white sofa.

Then he told me about the case he was working on — a young woman the press was calling "21st Century Mayflower Madam." That reference was to Sydney Biddle Barrows, who wrote a book back in the 1980s about her life as a madam with a fleet of call girls to the movers and shakers of the time. Her own pedigree put her among those founding families in the U.S. whose dirty laundry is usually kept entirely hidden. It turned out that Matt was her favourite of all her defence team, and he was hoping to use it to move himself into the spotlight for a promotion to partner in his firm. We couldn't have been more *Will and Grace* if we had shared accommodation, something he certainly did not suggest. We both knew that our friendship was predicated on a healthy dose of housekeeping distance.

Just before we hung up, I mentioned the odd note I'd found among the coffee bean bags.

"Read it to me," he said. When I was finished, Matt's response was blunt. "Sounds gay to me."

"How can you say that from just the note?"

"Just a feeling. Anyway, has it spawned another magazine article idea yet? Oh, I know," he said, "it's the plot line for the novel!"

"I'm still thinking about it. I guess I'll just keep it and hope that it inspires me."

Curiosity Killed the Cat: When Nosiness Leads You Astray

The note stayed on my little corkboard for the entire next week before I glanced at it again. I had been oddly occupied, although I can't say that I was busy. I certainly was not busy writing, but I had gone so far as to drift through a bookstore in town where I picked up a few things – in more ways than one.

You need to understand about bookstores in Cork Harbour — or should I say bookstore. There is only one, and it's no *Indigo* or *Borders* (probably just as well for business these days!). What I mean is that it is decidedly large for such a small town, but it is independently owned, just like in the old days, and the owners, Aurora Hudson and her husband Aristotle Cummings, were characters if there ever were two.

I had spent a lot of time in that bookstore in my earliest years in town after we moved there from the city. It was a kind of refuge for a nerdy girl who fancied herself a writer and who didn't have a lot of luck making friends. It was then that I developed my personal theory of baby names: weird names cause weird adults. There you have it. Aurora? Aristotle? I wondered whether either of them had a normal middle name that would have been better for public consumption. Years later, I looked them up on Google and found the answer: no. Aurora's middle name was Moonbeam, and Aristotle's was Meadow. At least things made more sense after that discovery. It seemed they were both products of hippie parents, and I'd venture to guess that Aurora's mother gazed at a moonbeam through the curtains as she gave birth underwater to little Aurora while Aristotle's mother crouched in a meadow, screaming her way through an unmedicated birth. But that was just my own idea; I never did work up the courage to ask either of them.

The truth is that they made the most dedicated bookselling team on the planet, and their hippie parents had evidently done well for themselves—rumour was that Aurora and Aristotle had been left millions, which is the reason they were able to afford all that independence from the mega-chains. This was much to our benefit in Cork Harbour, I'd have to admit.

The bookstore was large, warm and intellectually stimulating. Housed in a 19th-century brewery building, it occupied a pricey piece of waterfront real estate. In addition to an overwhelmingly diverse collection of books, they also sold art supplies: among the non-book items were notebooks of every kind you could imagine.

When I was in high school, I used to go in regularly to buy fancy journals to keep my most secret notes, always chasing an idea for a story. My particular favourites were *Moleskines*™. They were a brand created in the late '90s to bring back those notebooks that the Hemingway's and Picasso's of the world used in their day to keep now priceless notes and sketches. They came in a wide variety of fabulous colours, and I had tons of them in all different sizes. My father had complained more than once about this addiction I seemed to be suffering from since they were breathtakingly expensive compared to notebooks from the local drugstore. But the drugstore ones just weren't the same, I'd whined to him. How could I ever become one of the great writers of the world if I had to be confined to drugstore notebooks? That was then, and this was now. But my financial circumstances didn't seem all that different, nor did my deep-seated desire for them. So, I wandered the aisles of notebooks in the A & A Book Company (Aurora and Aristotle), running my hand over innumerable specimens of *Moleskine*™ notebooks, my hand coming to rest on the small purple and the large orange. So I bought them, and now they sat majestically on my grubby little desk in my little bedroom cave. I was determined to fill them with all manner of inspiring quotes and notes upon which I would base that novel.

However, while at the bookstore, I also sat down at the attached café, drank an espresso and ate a tuna salad sandwich. It turned out that the tuna salad had been ill-advised because I spent the next two days with my head in the toilet, resulting in several lost days and a seriously bad case of halitosis. I stayed away from work for the better part of the week. Lolling around in a cave has much to recommend it: when I wasn't head-in-toilet, I had time to think, a luxury that had eluded me almost completely sin—well, forever, or so it seemed.

Finally, I was feeling better, so I let my mind wander and wander it did. It wandered up the wall and onto the little note that was still tacked there. I was going to get up and throw it out when I was seized by the hand of curiosity. It was like it physically pushed me back onto the bed where I had been lounging in pyjama pants and a sweatshirt. (How the mighty have fallen!). *What if*—my mind started thrumming.

What if Juan Val Dez were a real person?

What if he were in trouble?

What if I could help?

What if he were handsome (Ricky Martin pops into my head – so what if he's gay)?

What if I could find him?

My malaise all but forgotten, I jumped to the computer and started searching. I started with his name. I found a couple of these Juans on Facebook, but one was from Florida and the other from Columbia; the latter, I suspected, was actually the fictional Juan. Not much help there. A Google search uncovered a lot about the fictitious Juan, so I started to think that a Juan Val Dez from Costa Rica might somehow be legitimate. It's funny how your mind draws these conclusions that defy logic when you want them to be so.

I flipped open the large orange notebook (I just knew that it was going to be money well spent) and started jotting notes.

Juan might be a real person who is somehow caught up in a situation beyond his control. He is reaching out to anyone. He is a prisoner on a coffee plantation. (A bit far-fetched, I know. Who takes hostages on coffee plantations? But I'm just getting started.) *He is a political prisoner.* (Do they even have political prisoners in Costa Rica? I've heard it's a great eco-tourism destination.) *He is caught in a love triangle.* (Where the heck did that come from?)

I chewed on the end of the pen I was using to jot my writer's notes on the acid-free paper of the notebook (they needed to be readable long after the great novelist was dead) and then surfed over to Wikipedia to read about coffee production in Costa Rica. I read through the statistics on the importance of coffee in the country's economy, the number of tons of coffee produced each year and the largest growing areas. I jotted them down: San José, Alajuela, Heredia, Puntarenas and Cartage. They all sounded so exotic. *Hmm... Could Juan be in one of those provinces?* Maybe I was getting somewhere.

Suddenly, I began to feel as if I were in some kind of spy movie. I was assigned to search for a missing political candidate or maybe a missing witness in an important trial, or maybe a jewel thief (where did that one come from?). Then it hit me.

I wasn't researching a possible novel storyline. I was researching a book about a Costa Rican who was reaching out to the world to help him deal with some kind of a problem that was beyond his control. It was my job to find him, help him and write a memoir about my adventures. That was it!

I stood up so quickly that I hit my head on the lamp that hung over the desk. Rubbing my head excitedly, I grabbed my cell phone. I had to share this with someone. I quickly texted both Matt and Faith and sat down to wait for someone to answer. It didn't take long.

When the phone buzzed, I glanced down at the small screen and wrinkled my nose. How odd, I thought, it was a text from Andrew.

"In Monte Carlo. What a crazy place. Miss u."

He was missing me? That was strange. I had not received a single message from him since the one inviting me to subscribe to his blog (he didn't seem to have picked up that I had already subscribed by then)—which he rarely updated, I have to say. There is nothing that bothers me more than people who start blogs and don't update them regularly (note to self: write an article or possibly a rant about bloggers missing in action). But I digress. Now he missed me? Well, I can't say that I was missing him any more than I was missing my urban lifestyle, of which he had been a small part. I was making up my mind to ignore his message when the telephone rang. I winced.

"So, when are you coming home?" Thank god it was Matt.

"Matt!"

"Okay, what exactly are you planning to do with this new-found rush of ideas? You're sounding perilously close to rash action."

"I'm not sure what's next. And hello to you, too." I was happy to be able to talk this over with Matt. The good old-fashioned telephone call is highly underrated in these days of instant messaging. "I'm thinking of going to Costa Rica."

I was as surprised by this verbalization as Matt was sure to be. I could only attribute it to another instance of failure to filter my thought processes, resulting in a public venting of my jumbled mind. I should have known by that point in my life that the results were usually not pretty.

"Are you crazy?" Matt yelled into the phone so that I had to hold the receiver away from my ear for a moment. "Pack your bags this minute and come back to Toronto. There must be something in the water out there—or you've eaten too much fish. You, Jenn Postman, are not the sort of woman who jets off without a plan to an unknown country to find an unknown man. Life is not a soap opera or a spy movie!"

Matt had a point.

"And if you need any more convincing, remember how much you like your stilettos and your lattes. From what I've seen of

Costa Rica and its eco-tourism activities, it's not the kind of place where there's a lot of stiletto-walking."

"Have you forgotten about the green polo shirt I'm now reduced to?" I said, looking at the little pile of three such shirts that were winking at me from the top of the dresser, just waiting for me to don one and toddle off to the gourmet grocery store to unload another carton of star fruit or dragon fruit or whatever Dad and Edward had ordered from some far-off land to keep their customers happy.

"All the more reason to pack up and move back to where you belong."

"There's that little matter of a job," I said. "And I have no apartment."

"I've given this a lot of thought, and I've decided, despite our agreement about the perilous nature of the situation, you can stay with me until you find something. And by the way, jetting off somewhere costs money. The last time we talked, you were moaning about suffering from its lack."

Desperate times call for desperate measures, or so we're told; this wasn't that desperate, at least not so desperate that Matt and I could be roommates any time soon. Moving in together, no matter how temporary, was not a good idea, and we both knew it. He was referring to the fact that more than once over the years, we had talked about sharing an apartment, but we always concluded that it would wreak havoc on our friendship. Both of us had always believed that a bit of real estate distance was essential to a good friendship—oh, heck, I thought that it was probably essential to a good relationship of any kind at that point in my life.

"Thanks for the offer. But you know that's not going to happen."

"Just promise me you won't do anything rash. And what about the money? And the time away from work? How do you think your father will feel when you say, 'Oh, by the way, Dad, I'm just flying off to Costa Rica?'"

My enthusiasm for the project deflated just a little as I thought a bit more rationally about it. I felt sure that Faith would echo Matt's thoughts on the subject. I guess I needed them both to ground me.

I chatted with Matt for a few more minutes and promised to plan a visit soon. It occurred to me that I really did need to get back there to begin a job search again, or the basement was going to become my permanent home. For some reason that I could not fathom, though, I wasn't ready to do that. I needed a plan.

About an hour later, I got a text message from Faith.

"Are you going to CR to find him?"

"Thinking about it," I tapped back. I thought I'd try the idea out on her, then braced myself for another outburst like the one I prompted from Matt.

"How exciting!"

Exciting? Faith thought it was exciting? I thought appalling might be the word she'd choose. But she thought it was exciting. It just goes to show you how still waters run deep or something like that.

I suddenly realized that I was bored; I needed to do something to assuage my curiosity. Then I remembered a quote that one of my writing professors in grad school used to have posted on her office door: "The cure for boredom is curiosity. There is no cure for curiosity." Dorothy Parker, I love you!

When Your Friends Surprise You

John Lennon famously wrote that he got by with a little help from his friends, so who am I to argue with Lennon? When I found out that Faith supported my as-yet-unplanned foray into the unknown, I glommed on to her like a baby koala clinging to a eucalyptus tree. Of course, as the idea of what to do next began to take shape in my mind, I knew that I'd need all the positive friend energy I could find – I knew that it was highly unlikely that I'd find any support among my family members unless I could figure out a way to make it seem like a terrific idea to them.

Maybe I could even get Dad to pay for it. Well, maybe that was stretching it, but I'm a lifestyle writer, and coming up with ideas is my stock in trade—or at least it used to be. But before I broached the idea of running off into the unknown, I thought I'd better do a bit of research. As it turned out, James was away at some gynecological conference (can you think of anything more boring?), so Faith invited me over for a girls' night. We were going to plot.

When I arrived at Faith's front door, with a wine bottle bag and potato chips in hand, she greeted me at the door with a bear hug.

"Okay, the coast is clear. James left for the airport three hours ago, and Flight Tracker says they're airborne now! So it's just us girls!" She was clearly excited about that prospect. I hadn't realized just how dull life as a doctor's wife in Cork Harbour must have been for her.

She already had her computer hooked up to the massive 62-inch television in the media room (some people really do have media rooms) and was surfing the net in full high definition. She also had wine and snacks and the telephone number of our favourite pizzeria at the ready as we settled down in the plush television-viewing seats. I was delighted that the pizzeria I had known and loved as a high school kid actually had delivery now!

"So, where do we start?" I was looking at the screen where a fantastic photo of a rumbling volcano greeted me.

"Well," she said, picking up the remote control in one hand and the computer mouse in the other, "you said Juan was in Costa Rica, so I thought we should get acquainted with the geography."

As we surfed through tourist websites, I started to have a little nagging feeling at the back of my skull. It was like a little person sitting on my neck whispering in my ear. It kept repeating, "You are crazy. You are crazy. You are crazy," in a kind of throaty whisper.

Was I crazy? Well, Matt certainly seemed to think so. In fact, it began to dawn on me that this was just as nuts as Andrew's knee-jerk response to his pink slip. I couldn't go running off into the unknown — or could I?

Matt was probably right. What was I thinking? I wasn't the kind of person who just took off on a whim. I was a planner. I made lists. I planned trips six months in advance. I had only ever gone on one vacation by myself. The year I finished grad school I had booked myself a Club Med vacation, as cliché as it sounded, and took myself off to Nassau in the Bahamas for a week of sun, surf and guys. There had been a great deal of sun and surf – I have never had such a bad sunburn in my life. But if there were guys, I didn't see them. The place was populated by families. How was I supposed to know that Club Med had morphed? Anyway, I spent most of the second half of the week slathered in aloe gel, slipping and sliding my way from the breakfast buffet to a shaded lounge chair and back to the buffet for lunch, with piña colada punctuation in between.

After that experience, I always did my research and planned. Well, wasn't that exactly what I was doing now?

"So let me see the note," Faith was saying as she poured the wine.

I came back to reality and rooted around in my purse until I found the now tatty, folded piece of paper. I was reminded of the article I'd written for *Vivacity* on how to figure out women's personalities from the contents of their handbags. I had interviewed a purse-personality expert. What surprised me most was that there were actually people who were purse-personality experts. The woman whose name I could not now remember had a Ph.D. in psychology and had done her doctoral dissertation research on just this issue. That was the time when I thought that I just might do a Ph.D. myself: after all, if you could get a Ph.D. in purses, well, the sky was the limit in my view. I had considered dissertation research on shoes until I found out that this wasn't a novel idea; people had actually already done it. I turned my attention back to Faith.

Faith shrieked as I smoothed the note out on the table. "Jenn Postman, you should be taking better care of that. It's the key to your future."

Okay, now I was starting to get scared. How could this down-to-earth, small-town-but-well-dressed doctor's wife be so drawn in by this piece of paper?

"Faith, what's the deal? I think you're more invested in this than I am."

Faith got up from where she was sitting on the floor and went over to the wall of cupboards that, much to my surprise, hid a wall of books. She took three of them off the shelves and brought them over. "Here are three of my favourites. But you see that wall of books? They're all mine." She smiled conspiratorially.

I took the three paperbacks from her and looked at them. Every one of them was some kind of mystery.

"I love, love, love a good mystery," she said, taking a long sip of wine as she sat down beside me again. "And if you think that bookshelf is full, you should see what's on my Kindle! Don't laugh, but I'm thinking of trying to write one."

Laugh? Why would I laugh? "Why would I laugh? If you want to write a mystery novel, then write one! It wouldn't surprise me if you beat me to publication."

"James thinks it's a stupid idea."

"Why did you even tell that bonehead?"

Faith looked at me aghast. My hand shot to my mouth as if such a gesture could keep in any more of these thoughts that were swirling in my head about her bonehead husband.

She sighed. "Well, I guess I can't expect you to like him when he doesn't like you."

It was her turn to put her hand over her mouth – as if I didn't already know that James didn't like me. After all, she had told me that he thought I was a bad influence. And really, what else can you conclude from a man who greets someone with the words, "What are *you* doing here?" It was only a small step from there to loathing in my mind.

She smiled a kind of lop-sided smile. "He is a bit of a bonehead, now that you mention it! And here's a list of coffee plantations," Faith was saying, changing the subject. She scrolled down a page in all its high-definition glory on the television screen in front of us.

I was suddenly reminded of one of Faith's most prominent talents: no one could deflect and/or change the subject under discussion as quickly as she could. In our youth, I'd often suffer from whiplash as she careened from one topic to another, blithely ignoring what she chose to ignore. I used to watch her do it with her mother when we were in high school. I usually just went along for the ride with her. So I figured I should just get with the program and get excited about the list moving right past her husband's completely unfounded (in my opinion) aversion to me – and his clearly evident boneheadedness.

"Here are three that offer tours. You could do that," she said, reaching for a pen and beginning to scribble down names. "What do you suppose the odds are that your guy is working on one of these? They seem like the big ones."

I took a sip of wine. "I hardly think I can refer to him as 'my guy.' But I guess it is possible that he works on one of these. Maybe I should start by seeing if the bags of beans in Dad's store have any information on them. You don't happen to…"

"…use *Café Exquisito*? Of course, I do!"

As Faith ran from the room, I realized that she was making my head spin. She was back in seconds, brandishing a half-used bag of the coffee beans in question. I knew I shouldn't have been the least bit surprised that she used the most expensive brand of coffee on the planet – or at least in Cork Harbour.

"I love this stuff. But the best thing about it is how it makes James complain."

I must have looked confused.

"He's so tight with his money he thinks we should buy only no-name brands at the supermarket regardless of how crappy they taste. He says if you're just going to imbibe it and no one knows about it, then you might as well go cheap. He just hates it when I shop at your father's store. I love it!"

I was beginning to worry about the state of Faith's marriage, but I'd get back to that another time. Faith's glee was contagious.

"It says here that the coffee is "single estate" coffee from…" She was trying to turn the bag around so she could see the address when the beans began to tumble out of the bag onto the carpet. I braced myself for a fit of hysterical cleaning. I was not to be disappointed in my expectation of hysteria, but it was more of the gleeful kind. She started laughing so hard I thought she'd spill her wine and everything else. Clearly, she'd had too much to drink. I was very grateful that James was currently winging his way toward that conference.

She started hiccupping madly as she smoothed out the now-empty bag on the floor. "Here it is. It says that the coffee is picked and roasted in some place called Puntarenas." With that piece of news, she expertly began typing the name into the search engine, not even trying to stifle the hiccups that threatened to overtake her at any moment.

In a nanosecond, there were over 10 million pages that came up on the list. "Wow," I said.

The salient information was that Puntarenas was both a city and the largest province in Costa Rica along the Pacific Coast. The pictures made me stop and stare. It was breathtakingly beautiful.

"Do you suppose it really looks like that?" I said as a particularly exquisite picture of a place called Manuel Antonio National Park came up.

I didn't know if it would be as beautiful in person, but I realized with a rush of clarity such that I hadn't felt in a very long time that I had to find out.

"I wonder how much it costs to fly to Costa Rica?"

The words were no sooner out of my mouth when Faith began madly typing "flights to Costa Rica" in the search engine. All I needed now was a plan for how I was going to break it to my father – oh, and one to figure out how to pay for it.

Why Everyone is Blogging and Why You Should Consider Stepping Away from the Computer

I'd like to think that I've been a writer ever since that day back when I was about eleven years old when I decided that there was no reason in the world why a pre-teen could not be a best-selling writer. That's about the time when the notebook obsession kicked in. If I had been born about ten years later, I would have been what the tech world likes to call an "early adopter"—in this case, blogging. Those little notebooks I had all over my bedroom were places where I wrote my most intimate thoughts and feelings. They were sometimes momentous, at least in my personal view, but as I look back on those notes, I can see that they were mostly vacuous. I sometimes wrote about ideas, but more often than not, I wrote things like: "I had bacon for breakfast today. I never eat bacon." "I just got back from the library. It was quiet there." "I just hate it when my English teacher picks apart Shakespeare." And so much more of that. It was clearly the kinds of things that you didn't share with anyone in the days before Twitter. At least we knew better than to share these things at that point—but you can see where I'm going with this.

So, perhaps I was saved from blogging by that abyss of time—those ten years—and I was saved from putting out there in cyberspace such inanities as clog the information channels these days. I know that I was saved from certain embarrassment, or worse, from some of the things I wrote. Like that time I was mortified in class by finding that I had come back from the bathroom with a trail of toilet paper stuck to the bottom of my shoe. The ragging I got from some of my so-called friends caused me to write the following in my little purple journal: "I'm going to smack Eileen's face if she ever laughs at me again." If I blogged or tweeted or "Facebooked" that today, someone's mother would have me arrested for threatening her daughter. Some things are best left in the privacy of a real journal that you keep to yourself.

Two days after my "research meeting" with Faith, I was sitting at my desk above the fruit aisle, thinking about how it was more likely that someone in my class would have snapped a photo of the offending toilet paper trail and posted it unbeknownst to me when my email pinged. Andrew had made a new entry on his blog. (Who was reading it, anyway? Other than me, of course.) Since I had subscribed to his blog every once in a while, I'd get an email with a link to his latest writing effort. In the last week, he had actually posted two updates. I'd inevitably click over to it to see the attached photos. I was so sure that I was uninterested in where he was and what he was doing, and yet I could not seem to stop myself.

He had been to Paris, the south of France, Italy, Greece, and now he was in North Africa. There was a picture of him standing in front of the entrance to the medina in old Tangiers in Morocco, wearing a pair of those zip-off pants that can become shorts and a T-shirt under what looked like a safari jacket of some kind – this from a man who once considered any shirt without a collar to be completely beneath his dignity. Well, that was back when we were a couple, anyway. The safari jacket was covered with pockets, and I could see a colossal camera dangling from a strap around his neck. I was astounded. Andrew used to make jokes about people who wore those travel-type clothes that could be rinsed out in bathroom sinks at night, and now here he was, looking like an ad for *Tilley Endurables*. And what was with that camera? His idea of photography had been clicking mildly embarrassing selfies and candids of his friends at bars with his iPhone. As far as I knew, he had never owned a proper camera and had never had the time or interest in taking real photographs. What was happening to him? And where was he getting the money for this junket of finding himself? I was reminded of that icky, narcissistic book *Eat, Pray, Love* that had provided the memoirs of a spurned and bitter woman taking a year to find herself by eating her way through Italy, praying her way through India and loving her way through—I don't know where because I couldn't finish it. Anyway, she didn't seem to have had much money to tide her over, but then she didn't seem to be the sort who cared about the thread count of her sheets like Andrew always had.

My eyes started to glaze over as I stared at the computer screen in front of me. Finally, my eye caught itself on the button beckoning me to start my own blog. Never, I thought. But my finger hovered over the mouse while I looked at his photo again. I was starting to get an idea.

"So I've been on the road for four months now, and I don't even miss the necktie. I'm thinking about going to India next. I'd like to spend some time on a kibbutz."

Dear god! Did he think that a kibbutz was in India? I started to write a comment on his blog entry and began to type, "Step away from the computer. Now. Before someone realizes that you're a dim-wit..." Then I thought about this for a few minutes longer and looked up at the top of his blog, where it said, "Not a member? Sign up now and start blogging."

And so I did. I signed up, and just like that, I was among those who needed to step away from the computer. I had failed to heed Matt's advice—again. I had only a momentary, fleeting thought that his advice was often sound.

So, why was it that now that I had decided to figure out a way to buy a ticket to Costa Rica to find my own bliss, as it were, I felt an overwhelming urge to open an account and start blogging—or should I say, blabbing—about it? Was I channelling Julie/Julia in the hopes of snagging a book contract from my as-yet-unwritten experiences? This was an unwelcome flight of ideas if ever I had had one. And Matt's voice was again ringing in my ear.

Now, I was staring right at a blank box with a caption that told me I'd have to name the blog. I sat back for a moment, and before I knew it, I'd called the blog *"The Unblog: The blog that isn't a blog at all."* I sat back and looked at the name, winking at me from the screen for a moment. *Yes*, I thought, *I do like that*. Now, however, I was faced with the yawning question of what the blog would be about. I could be like all of those zillions of bloggers out there who write about everything and nothing for no one – who reads all this stuff, anyway? Or I could put on my writer's hat and think about a thematic way to approach things. So, I started my first blog post. I called it *"Why you probably shouldn't blog."* This was for me. Here's what it said:

You, out there in blog-reader's land – wherever that is – I'm talking to you. You really shouldn't be reading this piece. You really should be doing something useful. Don't you have a life? [Who was I kidding? Who has less of a life: the blogger or the blogee? But that's for another blog post.] *There are lots of reasons why you shouldn't be reading this post, but I want to consider all of the reasons why I shouldn't be writing it. After all, it's my blog, and I'll write what I want to. So, here are my top ten reasons why I should not be blogging_and you shouldn't either.*

1. *Your family is bound to discover that there are things about them that you don't like but never meant to tell them. After all, families are great fodder for blogs. Just search for your name someday and see how many blog entries your family – near and extended —have mentioned you in.*

2. *You open up your life to every crazy person in the world who owns a computer hooked up to the web. I once wrote a story about blog-stalkers and what I learned should force me to stop typing right now, but I'm on a roll.*

3. *You open every decision you make in your life to criticism. If you can't talk about your decisions on your blog, what can you talk about? But for every person who agrees with you, there will be two*

more who think that you are (a) pathetic; (b) moronic, (c) depraved, (d) childish or all of the above.

4. *You are a crappy writer. Famous writer and teacher William Zinsser once wrote, "Most people have no idea how poorly they write." Amen to that, I say.*

5. *You've never had an independent thought in your life. No one likes a blogger who can only regurgitate what others have said. See my William Zinsser comment above. See what I mean?*

6. *You don't have time to blog. If you have ever (ever, ever) told someone that you're "busy, busy, busy," then you don't have time to blog. I once had a colleague tell me that he had "less than no time" to do something. It occurred to me that he had exactly the same amount of time that I had in a day: 24 hours. And yet, he had "less than no time." If you've ever said anything resembling this, you don't have time to blog. And you're too dumb to know that there's no such thing as less than no time.*

7. *Your life just isn't all that interesting to you. When someone asks you, "What's new?" do you ever say, "Not much," "Nothing," "Same-old," or some other variation? If you have ever said that, you are just not that into your life.*

8. *Your life just isn't all that interesting to anyone else. This is the key to it all. The truth is that no one really gives a flying f***k about your life. Everyone is so caught up in their own lives (about which they'll say that there is nothing new) that although a few of your friends will read your blog from time to time, they'll soon lose interest.*

9. *Your friends will tell everyone that your life is boring. This is really pathetic and should be avoided at all costs.*

10. *Finally, the mother of all of the reasons why you shouldn't blog is that no one will read it. What's that you say? You have a gazillion friends on Facebook? Two gazillion followers on Twitter? Well, come close, honey, and I'll tell you the bare-faced truth: I don't care if they are your followers, fans, friends or some other such technical term. They won't read your blog.*

So, there you have it. Time to stop all this blogging and go back to other, more interesting things—and when you come up with one, let me know. ~Jenn

So, what does this foray into blogging have to do with my decision to take a trip to Costa Rica on a whim with no idea of what I was doing, where I'd end up, how I would pay for it or who I'd end up with?

I sat back in my chair and picked up a cushion from where it had fallen on the floor earlier. I hugged it into myself and took a deep breath. I reached out for the mouse and clicked back to Andrew's blog photo, then over to my blog. I looked back at the photo and took a closer look at the camera. The camera was giving me an idea, but it was the wrong kind of camera. I needed a video camera and a YouTube channel.

I picked up my phone and texted Faith: *I have an idea.* Then I got ready for bed. By the time I had finished brushing my teeth, my phone pinged. It was a message from Faith.

I knew you'd come up with something! It said. *Breakfast at Tiffany's?*

Before you get all caught up in the Tiffany's thing, you need to know that Tiffany Smith-Jackson runs a chichi '50s-style diner in Cork Harbour. It's listed on all the "where-to-eat" websites.

Meet you there at 9 am, I texted back. I didn't have to be at work until 11 am.

I had no idea about the details of this idea, but I just knew it was going to be brilliant.

Blogging must be very tiring because that night, I slept better than I had since I moved back into my parents' basement. I got up early, showered, donned my newly pressed green polo shirt, over which I threw on a favourite sweater to cover up at Tiffany's, and then padded up the stairs for coffee. As usual, my mother had beaten me to it. She often painted *en pleine d'air*, as the French impressionists were fond of saying—actually in the fresh air— early in the morning. As I stepped into the kitchen, she was just coming in through the back door, wiping watercolour paint off two brushes in her hand.

"Good morning, Jenn," she said when she looked up. "You're up early. Adapting to the new position in life?"

"Sort of, Mom," I said as I poured myself a cup of coffee that she had obviously prepared before going out. It tasted as if she had been outside painting since before sunrise. I grimaced. "Mom, can I ask you a question?"

"Of course you can." Mom dumped the offending coffee in the sink and pulled out the bag of coffee beans – sure enough, they were from *Café Exquisito*. She poured them into the grinder and then into the coffee maker. The aroma of fresh coffee filled the large, sunny room. "Shoot."

"Huh?"

"What kind of question do you want to ask, Jenn?"

"Oh, yeah. Did you ever do something in your life that was really out on a limb? Really different from what people expected of you?"

"Where are you going with this?"

"I'll get to that. But, right now, I want to have a real conversation with my mom, the artist."

"Mom, the artist, huh? Not just Mom the mom?" She looked at me, but I didn't respond. "Okay. Let me think." She poured each of us a fresh cup of coffee and took them over to the kitchen table in the bay window that overlooked the water. "I'm not sure how out on a limb this is in the real world, but in my world, it was a bit of a deviation from the norm."

I looked at her as she took a sip of coffee, watching her face as she recalled an event. I waited patiently for her to continue.

"After I finished art school and tried to make it as an artist for two years, I applied to business school. I actually attended classes for six weeks in an MBA program."

I gasped. My mother in business school? My mother, the perpetual artist studying economics or whatever else they start with in business school?

"It was awful. The worst mistake I had ever made in my life. I learned that I needed to be true to myself and not go off doing stupid things that were so far away from my authentic self. Now, what do you really want to talk about?"

Mom had always been a very perceptive woman. I guess true artists have that as a part of their nature. When I was younger, it could be a great burden, though, since she always seemed to know me better than I knew myself.

"Oh, I just have an idea. I'll talk to you and Dad about it tonight." I rinsed out my coffee cup and put it in the dishwasher.

"Aren't you going to have any breakfast, honey?" Mom was always concerned with balanced nutrition. That's probably why she didn't look anywhere near her real age. I hoped it was genetics.

"Meeting Faith for breakfast."

"At Tiffany's?" She started to smile, and then we both cracked up. It was an old joke in Cork Harbour.

"Mom, could you do me a favour?"

She nodded.

"Could you and Dad be here at 8 o'clock this evening to discuss something with me?"

"Something?" she asked.

"Hmm. Yeah. Just…something." I smiled.

"Since you're smiling, I'm relieved. Okay. I'll have him available for a chat this evening."

I blew her a kiss.

How to Negotiate Your Way to Anything You Want

I suppose that deciding that you can negotiate anything is probably over-reaching. I just knew that I had a fantastic idea if only I could get my father to see it that way. So, as I always do when I begin planning a magazine article, I started some serious research on the fine art of negotiating. I needed some kind of a one-liner to get me started.

I was surfing the online book sites as I sat sipping coffee at Tiffany's, waiting for Faith. The names of the books were an education unto themselves: perhaps I wouldn't even need to read on. *Getting to Yes. Getting Past No. Getting More.* These were the things I had to be able to do before I let myself loose on Dad. As I was looking through all of this material, it suddenly struck me that I had made my first decision. I was going to go to Costa Rica.

Who knew that there were so many web sites, books and so-called experts in the art of negotiation? I didn't, but it was occurring to me through all this that I was in a perfect position now to start thinking about a freelance article on the subject, and I would focus on women.

By the time Faith arrived (fifteen minutes late, I might add, but I really didn't notice—she blamed it on traffic, but who was she kidding in Cork Harbour?), I had decided on not only an approach but on making my father an offer that he couldn't refuse.

We decided to order first and then get down to business. I perused the cute menu that was decorated with jewels, of course, my mouth starting to water at the very thought of pumpkin pancakes with ginger cream sauce and every sort of omelet known to man or woman. I stopped there and went back to the pumpkin pancakes. Faith ordered a ham and cheese omelet and we settled back into our leather-upholstered bench seats and savoured our cappuccino until the waiter arrived with our breakfasts. My stomach grumbled in anticipation when it caught a whiff of the extraordinary aroma of ginger in the air.

"You know what James said to me this morning?"

I couldn't even pretend to know what James might be saying or thinking. "James home already?" I said between bites.

"No. He called—he does every morning when he's away. Anyway, he said that I should spend less time with you. He said that you're a bad influence on me."

This again? Well, I couldn't argue the point. I was opening Faith's eyes to the realities of the world outside her claustrophobic marriage—but then, who was I to judge? But I didn't say any of that to her. I took another bite of pancake and mumbled something supportive.

"What did you say?"

She swallowed. "Only that you're doing fine."

She moved the omelet around on her plate for a moment as if contemplating something truly profound. "James wants me to go ahead and book that cruise for next month; I think he thinks it would be a good chance to get me out of town. And away from you. I can't think of anything I'd less like to do right now." She sipped her coffee before continuing. "I've decided I need a bit of space, so I'm going to go to Costa Rica with you."

What?" I was ecstatic! Faith and I together again – just the two of us. This was going to be the best adventure ever! Then, I had a sobering thought. This was serious business. "Have you told James about this plan yet?"

She shook her head. "No, but as soon as you hatch your idea—you haven't told me yet what it is, by the way—I'm going to put it directly to him. Either we have a two-week hiatus, or I can't be responsible for what might happen to our marriage."

"Are you really sure you want to do this? It seems like a drastic step." I stopped and looked at her closely. "There's something you're not telling me." Then I realized, to my utter shame, that I'd been so caught up in my own so-called problems that I hadn't even seen that my best friend in the world was having big-time problems of her own.

"Jenn, I have so rarely—and I mean maybe never—done anything drastic or even spontaneous in my entire adult life. It's only recently that I've..." She stopped and I thought better than to break into her thoughts. "Anyway, this will either put us back on track or..." She didn't, or couldn't finish this thought either, at least not out loud.

"Anyway, I don't want to talk about it right now—we'll get to it eventually," she said, finishing her eggs and delicately wiping her lipstick, which, by the way, had not even moved. "What I really want right now is to hear this brilliant idea."

I took a deep breath and set down my cutlery. I took a last sip of cappuccino and launched into the plan.

Faith agreed to come over to my parents' house at 8 pm after her evening telephone call from James. She also promised not to say anything to James – yet.

Later that evening at the appointed moment, with my mother being true to her word that she and Dad would be in the living room ready to listen, Faith rang the doorbell—for once, she was not late—and I ushered her in.

Dad was sitting in a deep wing-backed chair beside the massive beach stone fireplace. Mom was sipping her after-dinner coffee on one of the two plushy armchairs that faced each other across a large, low, square coffee table while flipping through an art magazine.

"They're here, Jack," she said, putting her cup on the table.

Dad looked up from his iPad, where I knew he was checking the stock market reports. "So, Jenn, what's this all about? A bit clandestine, don't you think, keeping us in suspense?"

Faith and I sat down on the other loveseat opposite Mom. Dad got up and joined her so that we were now two facing two. I opened up the file folder that I'd been holding under my arm and started to spread papers over the tabletop. *Okay*, I said to myself, *secrets to negotiating 101.*

I had done my homework as any writer would do. Then, I distilled all of that unmanageable information into three guiding principles:

1. Don't be too eager. (*This would be tough since I was bursting to get this done.*)
2. Don't be emotionally attached. (*I wasn't sure I could avoid this at all: It was emotions that led me to this plan in the first place*).
3. Don't let the opponent (*in this case, my father*) "write the contract" (*so to speak; this one I had to get right — it had to be my terms*).

Clearly, I was behind the eightball before we even sat down. But I was ready.

"As you know, Dad," I began as I laid out several charts in front of him, "your sales have been steadily increasing even in the face of the deepening recession." So far, so good. I had yet to tell him something that wasn't already patently clear to everyone in the room. "I wish I could take some credit for this, but you didn't really need me and my services to get you into the steady sales growth." I shuffled another piece of paper to the top. I cleared my throat — I was going to lose my audience soon if I didn't get to the point. "But as any businessman knows, growth can stall. It can stop or even reverse — not that I think you're on the decline. But I think that you might want to take another look at your customer engagement."

I thought I saw my mother's eyes start to roll back in her head. She was no fan of business-speak. This must have had her remembering her MBA classes.

"I have an idea that I think will put your business in the national — no international — spotlight." I stopped for a moment for effect.

"By some measures, I suppose it already is, but I'm listening," Dad said.

I leaned down under the table and pulled a brand-new video camera out of my bag. Laying it on the table, I started again. "I have an idea that will put your customers, and those who are not yet your customers, directly into the backstory of the food they eat. As you're aware," I had slipped into pitch mode and was on a roll, "there is an increasing interest in the provenance of food. Since you source your products from such interesting and ethical vendors, it would be to your advantage if they knew more about the stories behind their evening dinners. They could become virtual friends with the farmers and artisans who you deal with. So, I'm proposing a video channel consisting of the real stories of all of the people behind *Savoureaux*."

Dad picked up the glass of port that I hadn't even seen on the table and took a sip. "I suppose that you have an idea about how we might go about this project, economically, of course."

"Yes," I said, "I'm proposing a kind of pilot project. I think that you should start with the coffee that you import from Costa Rica."

"Okay," he said, "why the coffee?"

I picked up a spreadsheet in front of me and pointed to the sales growth figures. "In just the past year, your online coffee sales have risen 140%, the highest growth factor among all your online products."

"And I suppose that you should go to Costa Rica to do the videotaping."

He got me. I would have to tread carefully. "Well, Dad, I do have a considerable amount of experience in interviewing for magazine articles, so I think I'd be the logical choice. And, of course, I'll need an assistant..."

"Faith, of course," Mom added.

Faith smiled widely. "I'd be delighted to help, and it just so happens that I have a two-week space in my social calendar." She looked from Mom to Dad so sweetly I could taste the sugar. Ah, my BFF was surprisingly good at this.

"So you're proposing a two-week venture. What happens then?"

I almost held my breath—Dad seemed genuinely interested. And in all of this conniving to get my trip to CR funded, it began to occur to me that I might actually be onto something.

"Well, then we'd begin to shape the stories when we got back, edit them and then post them on a video channel. We could also find other ways to incorporate them into our social media channels that we already have set up. Then we'll pitch a story to a national news outlet."

Dad sat back on the loveseat and looked like he was seriously considering this cock-eyed proposal. Reminding myself not to appear too eager, I consciously held myself back from talking on and on.

"You might have something here," he said finally. "But I do have a caveat."

Uh-oh, I thought. *Here comes my opponent trying to write the contract.*

"You have to take Edward with you."

Edward? For a brief moment, I hadn't the slightest idea to whom Dad was referring. Then it struck me. He meant Edward, the fruit guy.

"Edward's a kind of fruit fanatic, Dad, not a coffee expert."

"Maybe," he said, "but Edward is also a professional photographer and high-level amateur videographer. Who do you think took all the photos on that web site of ours—the one that seems to be able to sell products to far-flung customers?"

Of course, this news of Edward's creative tendencies came as a bit of a shock to me: he had seemed so one-toned to me.

"That's a terrific idea, Jack," Mom said. "Edward will also be a kind of calming influence on you two girls." She kind of pursed her lips like she used to do when giving me curfew rules when I was a teenager.

And what about 'girls'? We were grown women, but to Mom, we were still the two teenagers who could get themselves in a whole lot of trouble. I didn't know quite what to say. Things had been going so well.

"That seems like a good idea," Faith said quietly. "Perhaps he would be good for us."

I hesitated for just a moment but was well aware that this was probably non-negotiable for Dad. It was his walk-away ploy. And I didn't want him to walk away. This was the most fun I'd had since I returned to Cork Harbour.

"Do you think he'll agree to go with the two of us?" I said finally.

"Oh, he'll go," Dad said. "I'm a bit of a negotiator myself, you know." He smiled.

Then, for probably the first time in my life, I shook hands with my father—and went off to book tickets. Costa Rica: here we come!

A Field Guide to Travel Prep: An Online Shopping Extravaganza!

I remember writing an article a few years ago about how vivacious people face risks. As you probably guessed, it was Eleanor's idea to focus on vivacious people (remember *Vivacity*?). Anyway, while I was doing background research, I stumbled upon something that George Patton had to say about risk and thought that he might have a few nuggets of wisdom on the subject. He did.

Patton is reputed to have told us to "take calculated risks. That is quite different from being rash." So, not being rash by nature, I liked the idea of calculated risks. On the occasion of our impending trip to Costa Rica, despite Matt's caution – which he continued to share—I felt strongly that I was taking a calculated risk. Little did I know how much calculating we three adventurers would be doing.

When I think about my bucket list, I realize I'm not like most people. It isn't filled with those dream trips—those 1001 places I need to see before I die. But it is filled with things that cost money.

When I started grad school, I had actually written out my list, and it looked like this:

- Own a Hermes Birkin
- Own a pair of Christian Louboutin shoes
- Drink a bottle of Grand Dame Veuve Clicquot champagne
- Buy a BMW

…well, you get the idea. I was so superficial and vacuous that it makes me gag when I think about it now. I also had "give money to hungry children," but I'm sure that was the result of seeing one of those television programs and feeling just slightly guilty about the items that took priority. I had no deep-seated altruism, it seems. But I'm happy to report that within a few years, I realized how very stupid that list was.

And that list was before I found the note and before I started planning that Costa Rican adventure. Was I really being enticed by the possibility of helping someone? Anyway, there were still a lot of details to be worked out. The first such detail was Edward.

Dad told us not to worry about Edward; he'd be delighted. I thought that delighted might be overstating just a bit, but Faith and I left it in Dad's more than capable hands to inform his loyal employee that he was being deployed to the wilds of a foreign country with the boss's daughter and best friend. When put that way, I figured that Edward would flat-out refuse. I was wrong.

The day after we brokered our plan with Dad was Saturday, my regular day off. Edward, however, was working that day, so Dad went into the store to have a chat. At precisely eight p.m. on Saturday evening, I received a text from Edward requesting a meeting on Sunday afternoon. I have to admit it was very formal and very foreboding. I texted Faith, who was, according to her return text, busy trolling online shopping sites for travel apparel and equipment. She agreed to meet Edward and me at the store's main office the next day at 2 pm. The store would be open and very busy at that time—I only hoped neither Edward nor I would be commandeered into working the floor. It was a dangerous place to meet from that perspective, but in the interests of finding a neutral and work-related venue, it seemed prudent. So we were off.

Later on Saturday evening, my iPad started ringing. I was pleased to see that it was an incoming call from Matt. As I clicked 'connect,' his handsome face filled the screen.

"So," he said by way of greeting, "when are you coming home—and have you dropped the Costa Rica brainwave yet? Or did you spin it into a book idea?"

Oh, how well he knew me. "As it happens," I said, "Dad is sending Faith along with me and one of his employees to Costa Rica to do a background story on his coffee supplier."

Matt started to laugh. "So, your father really bought it."

"It's a terrific idea for his business."

"And an interesting angle for Jenn to work, though, don't you think? Clever girl."

"Well, I do have an idea for a book. You know the old 'what if' game that writers play? What if a lowly grocery store worker finds a note in the coffee shipment, and the note's writer is really in some kind of trouble? What if she decided to take action?"

"And she gets herself embroiled in a dastardly plot to overthrow the government of some god-forsaken country in Central America. But do you seriously think you'll be able to find this Juan?"

I had considered that long and hard. "I suppose it'll be a long shot."

"Like looking for a needle in a haystack, I'd say."

He wasn't telling me anything I hadn't already thought about, but something inside told me that this was a road I had to pursue. I had no idea why. I suppose deep down, I thought of it as a kind of epic love story where the journey is the main thing.

"Seriously, Jenn, have you really thought this through? If you do find him—and that's a big if—what if he turns out to be a drug dealer or worse? What if he exploits women?"

"If he does, then he's the dumbest criminal I've ever heard of. Putting a note in a coffee shipment wouldn't be a very viable business plan."

"No, I'd have to agree with you there. Anyway, who is this employee of your father's who's going with you?"

"Edward."

"Edward the fruit nerd?"

Evidently, Matt had been listening to me when I whined to him over the digital waves about Edward and his odd ways.

"Yes, the one and only."

Matt was laughing uproariously now. "Why him?" he finally managed to say between eruptions of laughter.

I ignored his amusement. "According to Dad, Edward is something of a video superstar. He knows his way around a camera."

"Maybe you and Edward were destined to be together."

I rolled my eyes. "Well, at least we'll have Faith to chaperone."

We spent a few more minutes discussing Faith and her evident marriage difficulties, Matt's newest cases and the social events I was missing in Toronto. Then we signed off, promising to keep in close touch as the trip plans progressed. We were scheduled to leave in three weeks.

I slept better that night than I had in ages.

The following day, Faith arrived on my doorstep—or more precisely, my parents' doorstep—with her laptop tucked under one arm and her black Mulberry Bayswater bag in the crook of the other.

"Okay," Faith said as she slid into a kitchen chair, "time to get to work."

"Work? We don't have to meet Edward for hours."

"Prep," she said, putting the laptop on the kitchen counter, opening it up and clicking furiously.

I coaxed Faith from her perch on a kitchen bar stool with a tray of coffee and biscuits from Dad's store – Faith's favourites. She picked up the laptop and followed me to the den, where we finally had some peace and quiet away from Emma, who had come into the kitchen to troll the refrigerator.

"Okay, Faith, what kind of prep are we doing this morning?" I sat down in the large, overstuffed sofa and put my feet up on the coffee table while biting into a biscuit.

Faith had taken up residence at Dad's massive oak desk and was absent-mindedly chewing while looking seriously at a web page open in front of her.

"Wow," she said finally, "there are a lot of sites for travel gear."

"Travel gear? What kind of travel gear?" I got up and walked over behind her to look over her shoulder.

"You know. Clothes, day-packs, flashlights, earthquake blankets…"

"Earthquake blankets?"

"Well, Costa Rica is on a fault-line, you know, Jenn. Can't be too careful. I was looking at a seismic hazard map yesterday."

"A seismic hazard map? What in the world is that?" For the first time since I had found the note, I was beginning to have second thoughts about this trip.

"Don't worry. There hasn't been a big earthquake in about five years. Only forty people died at that time anyway."

I could not believe that Faith seemed to be so blasé about the notion of fatal earthquakes. Perhaps I didn't know my best friend as well as I thought I did.

"I've made a list of things we'll need. I set up a wiki for us so that we can all contribute. I've just sent you the link." She looked up at me. "Don't you have your tablet or phone here?"

I didn't. "Why don't you read me your first draft list?" I figured that since it had been my idea to rope everyone into this, the least I could do was relinquish some control over the preparations. Anyway, Faith did seem to be having fun, and she was nothing if not organized and thorough. Thoroughness was not my forte. Perhaps if it had been, I'd have had a freelance writing career up and running before I lost my job. I digress.

"Okay. Here goes: rain ponchos, hiking boots, sun hats, sunscreen, insect repellent." Faith looked over at me. "Are you listening, Jenn?"

I was sort of listening. I was with her on the sunscreen stuff and the rain gear—I had heard it rains a lot in Costa Rica. "Continue," I said, sipping my coffee and thinking about Juan, whoever he was.

"Mosquito netting."

I sat up a bit.

"Disposable underwear."

I sat up straight.

"I draw the line there. Disposable underwear? Why do we need to dispose of our underwear?"

"Well, I figure that we don't want to be doing daily washing and who wants to take 14 pairs of underwear?"

It seemed logical, but I was now starting to think about her other items. Mosquito netting? Where did she think we were going?

"And, of course, we'll need day packs, and I found the most adorable safari jackets with matching zip-off pants."

I was beginning to get the picture. Faith was our rainforest stylist, and we were going to be the ultimate tourists. "I was sort of hoping to blend in a bit more."

"Don't worry. The safari jackets come in several colours, all of which will blend with the territory. I found a site that matches the clothes to the location. This is so fun!"

That wasn't actually the kind of blending in I had been hoping for. By the time we were finished, Faith had ordered a load of new stuff and posted her findings on the wiki, which apparently Edward had actually joined since she emailed him the link earlier. I shuddered to think about what he might say when we saw him later.

Once Faith had finished up all of her lists and made a couple of actual purchases, she packed up the laptop with great efficiency. "Okay, Jenn. Let's go meet Edward."

I looked at my watch, and she was right—we had just enough time for a lipstick break and the ride to the store.

When we arrived at the store, it was an ordinary Saturday—the place was packed to the rafters. Dad's usual piano player was suspended on a huge shelf above the coffee offerings, playing honky-tonk while the customers milled around, exclaiming over the freshness of the produce. It did bring a smile to my lips. Dad knew what he was doing all right!

Edward was perched half-way up the spiral staircase leading to the offices upstairs. When he saw us, he beckoned us over and then disappeared up the stairs. We followed.

He was ensconced in his tiny office with papers covering every imaginable inch of space and notebooks piled at the corner of the desk. I was thrilled to notice that they were the same Moleskines I favoured. Perhaps we did have more in common than I thought. I could almost ignore his safari-style jacket and neck scarf as if he were already dressed to embark on a dusty road trip. To be clear, I didn't think it would be all that dusty in CR since it is known more for its wet than its dry climate. As I looked around, I also noticed that there were several official-looking cameras and a large microphone covered with a fuzzy sock on a long handle like the ones I'd regularly seen held by man-on-the-street interviewers in downtown Toronto in my former life.

"So, where would you girls like to start?" he said, nodding at me and smiling at Faith. I was the boss's daughter; Faith was the customer/client/guest.

Scratch that notion of us having anything in common. Any man who refers to grown women as 'girls' has very little in common with me, my inner feminist was saying loudly in my ear. I chose to ignore her and at least keep my mouth shut.

I pulled out my notes. "I think we need to consider our objective first."

Faith cleared her throat a bit too loudly, in my estimation. I ignored her as well.

"Our objective, as you know, is to capture the backstory of the coffee producers whose products we carry."

"I think it's fair to say that we don't want to waste your father's money," Edward said.

"Naturally. Where are you going with this?"

"Of course, we're going to get to the coffee plantations, but I think it would be remiss of us to miss the opportunity to scout out some new and exotic fruits. Did you know that Costa Rica is home to a wide variety of exotic fruits?"

"Yes," Faith said a bit too eagerly. "I did some research. You are so right. This store could be the go-to place for the newest and trendiest fruits."

Edward beamed. I thought that we were straying a bit too much from my—our—objective. Coffee plantations were the priority.

"I'd like to see if we could source zapotes and water apples." He handed us each a photo.

The zapotes looked like small squashes with large, central pits. The water apples, on the other hand, looked like a cross between a pear and an apple – pear-shaped, apple-coloured. I momentarily wondered what they tasted like.

"Okay," I said, "we'll try to find some of these, but let's not lose sight of our priority. Coffee plantations."

We spent the next hour discussing flights, hotels and luggage. Edward was uncommonly pleased by the notion of the wiki for our collaborative preparations. It seems that he was also something of a social media buff, although he had never mentioned this to me.

By the time we had finished, we had booked plane tickets and considered hotels and drivers/guides. We didn't book the latter two, though, since Edward informed us that Dad had told him he'd look after these two items. Maybe he had a few business contacts, I thought. We also ended up with a tentative itinerary and a list of places we'd have to contact before we left. I offered to be the first contact with the coffee plantations, Edward with the fruit growers.

We said our goodbyes, and then Faith and I started down the stairs. "That was the most exciting thing I've done in years," she said, smiling. Then her smile drooped. "Now all I have to do is tell James I'm not going on the cruise with him."

She hadn't told him yet? Geesh.

How to be a 'Good' Tourist

The weeks slipped by quickly, and we were finally ready to leave. Faith had told James—well, I'm not exactly sure what she told him – and his reaction notwithstanding, nevertheless, she was there the morning we left, waiting on her front doorstep dressed head to toe in gear she had clearly ordered online from a retailer that must have been called "Clothing-With-Lots-of-Pockets" or something to that effect. She had her high-end, black nylon day pack swung across her body and her suitcase at her side when I pulled up in the taxi.

Faith had taken the rainforest-trekking/eco-tourism idea to heart: her outfit consisted of a crisp, dung-coloured safari jacket that would have put me in mind of those hemp, drawstring pants that did in the Birki experiment at *Vivacity* if it hadn't been for the fact that the whole outfit was crisp, immaculate and had knife-like creases in the front of the travel pants and down the sleeves of the jacket. She was sporting a Tilley raffia fedora that she explained was fashioned of tea-stained Madagascar raffia, affording her an SPF of fifty+. Whatever.

I was wearing a pair of black yoga pants, sneakers (they were cute ones, though), and a jacket I used to wear back in the days when I was a devoted running fanatic (thankfully, that phase had passed). I had a baseball cap that I'd picked up on a trip to Hawaii (thus had a Hawaii logo and palm tree on the front of it) in my carry-on bag. She looked like an ad for a chic eco-travel company. I looked like a reject from a South American youth hostel. What was happening to me?

There had been a time when I would never have considered the possibility of boarding an airplane without ensuring my outfit was fashion-forward, comfortable, and appropriate should I happen to meet someone important: a potential employer, possible story subject, potential boyfriend, or even more important, an old boyfriend. And now I was reduced to yoga pants in public! Perhaps it was indeed time I moved back to the big city. At least I still had my LV carry-on.

When we arrived at the check-in counter at departures, Edward was already there waiting. He was travelling light, to say the least. He had a backpack and nothing else. I thought that, unlike Faith, he planned to wear the same outfit regardless of the occasion. Oh well. I only hoped he'd be helpful and not too odd.

We flew first to New York, where we were connecting to Miami and then onward to San José. When we arrived at the boarding gate at JFK, a sullen morass of the travelling public was sitting miserably on their bags. Boarding didn't seem to be in the offing, although it was just 35 minutes to flight time. It seemed that the flight was over-booked. *So what else is new*, I thought. Well, the situation was that unless someone — correction, six someone's – agreed to give up their seats, no one was leaving. Six airline staff members were standing up at the counter, arms folded with their bags awaiting their freed-up seats. Over the next half an hour, the announcements from the agent at the counter slowly upped the ante. Flight time came and went and only three people had offered up their seats. It was now clear to us that we would almost certainly miss our connection out of Miami with all of the domino-like events that occurred as a result of missed connections.

"You know what we should do," Faith was saying as she scrutinized her boarding pass. "We should offer to stay."

"What?" I was dumbfounded.

"Give up our seats," she said.

Edward now looked up from his phone.

"Think about it," she said as she started to put her bag over her shoulder. "They're offering dinner, a night in New York and an upgrade tomorrow. It will be great."

"But we have a connection. They're not likely to be able to fix that," I was saying. "We'll miss our flight from Miami to San José."

"Fear not," she said, winking and making her way to the counter.

Edward and I stood there uncomprehendingly as Faith approached the counter where an attractive male agent was awaiting just such a development. We watched as they chatted for a moment or two. Finally, she beckoned us over to the counter. Edward looked at me, shrugged, then swung his backpack over his shoulder and headed toward Faith. I picked up my LV bag and followed them.

Faith had indeed wangled our seats on the next day's flight from Miami to San José – and in first-class no less! As anxious as I was to get to our destination and embark on my little adventure, I was a tiny bit thrilled about an evening in a big city. I was missing Toronto more than I cared to admit. So I called the hotel in San José and our driver, who would meet us at the airport (Dad had provided his contact information), to tell them that as a result of flight delays, we would be a day late. With arrangements made, new boarding passes for the next day and hotel vouchers in hand, we were off to Manhattan for the evening.

"You are amazing, Faith," I was saying as the taxi crossed the East River. "I thought for sure they would offer a hotel at the airport."

She giggled slightly. "They did," She said, "but I convinced them that they should put us downtown."

That's all she would say. Edward, who was wedged in beside us in the back seat—the driver wouldn't let anyone sit upfront with him on the other side of the glass barrier—was surprisingly in tune with this new adventure. I had thought that he'd be furious, so intent he seemed to be on getting to Costa Rica and embarking on his fruit and coffee assignment.

"There's a Gourmet Garage close to the hotel, so I think I'll head over there to check out the competition."

"I hardly think that a gourmet grocery store in New York City is any competition for Dad's little shop."

"I guess you haven't checked our online customer database recently," he said, tapping something on his phone. He turned the screen toward me.

Much to my surprise, he had the database – in its entirety – on his phone. He was nothing if not dedicated to his job.

"As you can see," he said, scrolling through the list, "we have a vast number of cross-border customers, and large numbers are right here in New York. Not sure why, but if I get a look at some of the local spots, I might get a handle on it."

I was impressed, to say the least. I was beginning to think that Edward was a bit of a dark horse.

After checking into the hotel, Edward took his camera and headed off to explore the grocery store, promising to meet us for dinner in a couple of hours. Faith and I looked at each other and started to giggle furiously. We were together in a big city with no commitments. I can't imagine what it felt like for Faith, who had spent her adult life in a sleepy seaside town, but for me, it was a feeling that I hadn't had for a very long time. We immediately set out to find a cocktail bar, after which Faith said she just had to visit Saks for a high-end fix and Century 21 for a low-ender. I was on board—despite my lack of clothing funds.

Several hours later, when we met Edward back at the restaurant in our hotel, we were more than a little buzzed, and not just because of the two or three champagne cocktails Faith had insisted on buying us at a cute wine bar we happened to pass on our way back. When we arrived, shopping bags in hands, Edward was already sitting at a table set for three, his face hidden behind the large menu, when we spotted him from the entrance. The hostess led us over to him, and we were able to maintain our dignity until we sat down.

"Have you two been drinking?" he said, putting the menu on the table. "Is this the way the trip is going to go?" He sounded like an exasperated father.

"Oh, Edward, chill a bit. We promise not to drink every day." I hiccupped. "At least not too early in the day."

After his reaction to our happy state, I was surprised when Edward insisted on ordering wine with dinner since I had always pictured him as a tea-totaller. It seems that he did, indeed, have outside interests and skills. He expertly discussed several bottles with the sommelier and Faith, who seemed a bit of a wine enthusiast herself, before settling on a reasonably priced bottle, but what turned out to be an exquisite bottle of Shiraz that complemented our dinner impeccably. I was so impressed that I wanted to ask him where he had gained such wine knowledge, but he wanted to charge ahead with our trip plans.

Our dinner conversation stuck pretty much to the job at hand — I still had not mentioned to Edward that I was on a secret mission to find one Juan of the coffee plantation and hadn't yet decided if I ever would mention it. Did he really need to know? I was certain that he'd think me a fool, although I wasn't entirely sure why I cared what Edward thought I did. Deep down, I guess I thought myself a bit of a chump, too. I didn't need anyone to point that out to me. Anyway, Faith kept us both mesmerized by the sheer volume of the research she had done for this trip. I know I'll go to feminist hell for this, but I think that Faith's skills were being wasted as a stay-at-home wife, although she had told me several times that it was her choice. Come to think of it, she seemed to protest that state a bit too much. I'd have to remember to talk to her about it.

"Just look at that," Faith said as she finished her key lime pie.

Edward and I both looked in the general direction in which she was gesturing with her napkin. I didn't have a clue what she was talking about.

"Just look at those shoes," she said.

Then I spotted them. I was reminded of a piece I had written for *Vivacity* about North American tourists, with a special emphasis on the American part. There they were: the poster children for the typical tourist. Several tables over sat a couple, probably in their mid-forties, not old by my standards, sporting huge white sneakers and fanny packs. Good lord! Wasn't there a law banning fanny packs yet?

"When will people learn," she said. "Don't they know that those shoes simply scream 'ugly American'?"

"They might be Canadians," I said quietly.

"Canadians? Are you serious? No Canadian in her right mind would be caught dead in enormous bright, white sneakers on foreign soil." Faith drained her wine glass ceremoniously.

"I do have to point out that if they are Americans, which given our current location is very likely," Edward ventured, "then they're not on foreign soil."

Faith wiped her mouth daintily with her linen napkin. "Oops," she giggled a bit. "Sorry about that. Of course not." She peered at the offending sneakers and their owners once more. "Good heavens, maybe they *are* Canadians!"

By the time we had finished dinner, we were all laughing about our upcoming research trip—well, perhaps not all of us. Edward managed to crack a smile in response to Faith's attempts to get him laughing, but that's about as far as it went. I was beginning to think that it was going to be Faith's mission to crack that geeky façade.

We said our good-nights and slept soundly in the luxurious beds that are such ubiquitous marketing features of upscale hotel chains these days. Then, we were up early to make our way to the airport once more. This time, there didn't seem to be any overselling issues, and we made our Miami connection easily. With our upgrades to business class on the New York to Miami leg, we thought we were in heaven—then Faith managed it again, and we found ourselves dining off porcelain and drinking Californian Chardonnay en route to Costa Rica as well. I don't know how she managed it, but neither Edward nor I were going to complain.

Needless to say, by the time we landed in San José in the early evening, we were feeling nicely buzzed.

Genius or Insanity: Finding that Fine Line

Mostly I hate Twitter, but occasionally someone tweets a quotation or a *bon mot* that resonates with me. Matt once tweeted a quote from American Elbert Hubbard, who seemed to have several folksy but erudite things to say at the turn of the twentieth century. The one that fluttered across my mind as the plane banked and readied for touchdown was this: "Genius may have its limitations, but stupidity is not thus handicapped." *Hmm*, I wondered, *what was the stupidity quotient in my fixation on Juan?* I guess I would find out soon enough.

American Airlines flight 2230 touched down at the Juan Santamaria International Airport in San José five minutes before its scheduled arrival time of 8:30 pm. We whisked easily through immigration and customs, then made our way to the arrivals bay to search for our names among the many white placards being held out by drivers of various stripes.

I finally spied what I presumed to be our driver in the sea of bored-looking drivers waving placards. His white lollipop sign said, "Welcome *Savoreaux*."

I beckoned to Faith and Edward, and together, we walked over until we were almost in front of him. He immediately dropped his sign to embrace Faith like a long, lost daughter.

"Señorita Postman, it is so wonderful to finally meet you! I have heard so many pleasing things about you from your great father!"

First, he was hugging Faith. Second, I had no idea Dad even knew anyone in Costa Rica. It seemed to have slipped his mind when I was negotiating for this little junket. And third, why in the world would this man know anything about me at all? I cleared my throat while Faith smiled over his shoulder at me and whispered, "I told you that you should have dressed better."

When Faith was finally able to extricate herself, Señor Mezza, as he introduced himself, was set straight about who was whom. He laughed heartily and immediately threw his arms around me.

"I should have known. You have your father's eyes!"

My father's eyes? Señor Mezza had met my father? This was getting very peculiar. I stepped back to take a closer look at Señor Mezza. He looked to be about Dad's vintage, with cropped salt-and-pepper, curly hair. He sported a large, floppy mustache, equally as salt-and-pepper as his hair. He was short—about my height, a bit stocky, like a former wrestling champ gone to seed. He was wearing an impeccable white, linen, long-sleeved shirt flowing outside of a pair of black, crisply pressed trousers and bare feet in leather slides. He smelled faintly of Old Spice aftershave. Where in the world had he met my father?

Now that I thought about it, Dad had insisted on finding us a driver/guide himself, and on personally booking our accommodation. I knew that we were to spend the first night at a Marriott Hotel not far from the airport—he had so many loyalty points that I figured we'd be staying at Marriott properties exclusively. I had hoped for a bit more of an authentic Costa Rican experience, but who was I to argue with a king-sized bed topped with the most comfortable mattress toppers in the industry? Instead of writing a magazine article about B and B's in CR (see, I did have real freelance writing dreams!), I'd write about the mid-luxury experience—or something like that. I'd have to work on the angle.

I continued to puzzle about Señor Mezza's prior knowledge of my father (and of me, it has to be said) as we followed him to his waiting van, which would be our daily transportation for the next two weeks. Dragging both my suitcase and Faith's behind him (we had insisted we could manage them; he had insisted more vociferously that we would do nothing of the kind), he chatted amiably with Edward as they both made their way out the exit door into the twilight and heat of the San José evening.

I breathed deeply. I had been to the tropics a few times before in my life, and the thing that got to me every single time was emerging into that sultry air. San José was blessed (I guess) with a modern airport that used jetways into the terminal rather than letting the passengers out onto the tarmac. Whichever way you experienced it, the first moment enveloped by the steamy air was always one to savour. After that single moment of enjoying the air, I had to scramble to keep up with the little parade. Then it struck me: we were in Costa Rica! The distance between Juan and me was diminishing by the moment. I was giddy with excitement—or, perhaps, a touch of lunacy exacerbated by the free wine aboard the flight.

The drive to the hotel was short: after all, it was located some 28 kilometres from the actual city! There would be no strolling around the plazas in the moonlight. We'd be having a late dinner at the hotel and mapping out the journey that we would embark upon early in the morning. I was excited.

At eight am the following morning, Edward knocked firmly on the door of the room I was sharing with Faith. She was still putting together travel outfits that would be suitable for what Señor Mezza had told us would be a fairly rough three-and-a-half to four-hour drive to Manuel Antonio on the west coast. This bit of information puzzled me since I had looked up the driving distance on the map and had figured that it shouldn't take us more than an hour and a half. It was less than 60 kilometres, after all. When I had mentioned this to Señor Mezza as he dropped us off with the hotel bellman, he simply smiled and said, "You are not in Nova Scotia any longer, dear Jennifer."

Edward had also smiled somewhat patronizingly. What did he know that I didn't?

Anyway, when I opened the door to tell Edward that we'd be another fifteen minutes, he was standing there in his own version of one of Faith's safari outfits or bushman's outfits: I could picture him in the outback in Australia herding sheep—but with clean, well-pressed clothing. His hat was one of those waxed canvas types that reminded me of *Raiders of the Lost Ark*. I stifled a snicker.

"You're laughing at my hat, aren't you, Jenn?" he said.

"No, no, I'm not, really." It did look kind of good on him in a geeky kind of way. But I was still stifling a giggle.

Faith peeked around the door, still in her bathrobe but fully made up with mascara, blush and lipstick. I was wearing only lip gloss. My fastidious city-slicker style seemed to have deserted me.

"I think it looks cute," she said. "In fact, I have one just like it!"

Dear god, I thought, they *match*. This was a touristic nightmare in the making. The only saving grace was that neither of them was sporting white sneakers. Faith did have her rules.

Edward smiled. "Thank-you, Faith. And you'll regret not having one when we get on the road, Jenn." He rearranged his backpack and told us he'd meet us downstairs for breakfast in fifteen.

By the time we joined him in the dining room, he had already taken the liberty of ordering for us. I wasn't sure if this presumptuousness miffed me or secretly flattered that he was trying to look after us—as if we needed looking after. I decided I'd wait until after seeing what was on offer before coming to any hasty conclusions about his questionable motivation.

As we sat down, a beautiful young tica—Edward informed us that this was the proper term for people from Costa Rica—materialized from nowhere with a pot of steaming coffee in one hand and an equally hot pot of steaming milk in the other.

"*Café con leche*," Edward said as she poured the coffee halfway up the cup and then filled it to the top with milk.

One sip, and I knew that I had reached coffee nirvana. Why had no one ever told me that this was the way to drink coffee? All those *grandé moccachinno macciato latte* blah blah's that I'd pretentiously ordered over the years, and this was what real coffee tasted like. I was going to like touring coffee plantations in Costa Rica.

After a few silent sips around the table, the waitress put plates of what Edward then explained was the typical Costa Rican breakfast in front of us. Now, I am a breakfast eater, but toast or cereal with skim milk and coffee is all I'm able to manage. This looked like dinner. In the United States. Where the serving size is as big as the smiles at Disney World.

I thought Edward was going to tuck his snowy linen napkin under his chin and dig in, but he picked it up, placed it nicely on his lap, and proceeded to dig in with table manners that would have made the Queen proud.

"*Gallo pinto*," he said between mouthfuls.

Faith was peering at her plate with a face that was a cross between this-is-interesting-but-odd and I-think-I'm-about-to-puke.

"*Gallo pinto*, you say?" I said as I held my fork tentatively over the massive mound of food.

"Rice and beans with scrambled eggs, chopped beef, and fried plantains. And those are the tortillas," he said rather unnecessarily. They were the only part of the breakfast that I recognized. Although I have to say I almost didn't since they were so out of context at this hour of the day in this venue. I should have been stuffing them with refried beans while sipping a Margarita.

So we dug in and enjoyed every bite. Costa Rica was getting better and better by the minute.

An hour later, at nine a.m. on the dot (Edward insisted on punctuality—Eleanor would have loved him for that), we shuffled, bag and baggage, out to the portico to await Señor Mezza. As it turned out, he had been there for some time and was deep in conversation with one of the bellmen, whom he seemed to know rather well. We would soon come to find out that he seemed to know almost everyone in the country rather well.

"You are all well?" he asked. "You have slept well under our beautiful skies?"

We nodded in unison.

"Good. And did you take a hearty breakfast?"

We nodded enthusiastically.

"Oh, well," he said as he heaved our suitcases into the back of the van, "perhaps that will be all right. A full stomach *might* be a settled stomach."

What did he mean by that?

The Authentic Travel Experience:
Not All It's Cracked Up to Be

A few months before *Vivacity* folded, Eleanor had mused about the notion of experiential travel and how it might make a good feature piece if we had the money to send one of us out for what she called an "authentic travel experience." The way she waxed rapturously about the "authenticity" of staying off the beaten path, of getting to know the "real" people and places of the world, almost made us want to volunteer. Almost. She then proceeded to circulate a series of photos from blogs of individual "authentic" travellers to whom she subscribed. *Mother of god*, I thought at the time, *I think I prefer the Marriott*.

The "authentic" travel experience evidently consists of staying at rat-infested, decaying hostels, touring city slums and eating highly questionable street food. Well, I suppose that a certain amount of "authenticity" can be experienced that way. Still, I always like to think that there is a different side to "authenticity"—a side where people in other countries weren't really so different from me. I was interested in that side where I could stay clean and avoid dysentery. I remember reading an article by a woman travelling in Samoa who was disappointed that the Samoans had televisions. She didn't think that it was authentic! And how dare they have internet! It was the ruination of her "authentic" experience. Phooey. I just wanted to tour coffee plantations. But getting there—that would be authentic, it seemed.

Señor Mezza expertly navigated the van out of the Marriott parking lot and onto the highway. Soon, we were sailing along, admiring the greenery waving in the breeze. And there was a lot of greenery. He had made an itinerary for us and would not be swayed from it. As we left the city environs, the road became narrower and the vegetation denser, but the driving speed never changed.

We were fascinated by the beauty of the countryside but even more mesmerized by the roads! Señor Mezza had not been kidding about the need for a full stomach. After we left the environs of San José, the capital, we zipped onto the highway – and I use that word very loosely—that was paved and, in some places, reasonable. In others, primarily where the highway crossed rivers, it was not reasonable. Not at all.

"Close your eyes," Señor Mezza told us as we approached the first of several "bridges." I, of course, use the term bridges loosely. In Canada, they would have been called precarious-boards-over-crocodile-infested-gorges. In Canada, there would have been some sort of local protest – in a civilized Canadian sort-of way—after which the bridge would have been summarily closed until it could be repaired to standards of safety that were clearly not on the books here. But that was there, and this was here, so we closed our eyes. Although I did peek a few times, just enough to be convinced that I would rather not see what was coming should one of the boards give way. The crocs looked hungry to me.

Our stomachs had been joggled and jostled for two and a half hours by the time we made our first stop at an off-the-road gift-shop-snack bar whose proprietor was evidently a friend of our amiable driver.

A petite woman who spoke not a word of English, Fabia might even have been Señor Mezza's wife for all we knew and observed, although neither of them was saying. She wagged her finger at him for some unknown reason, then said something that, if my rusty, high school Spanish could be trusted, sounded like an admonishment for being late. I wondered how late we were. When she led us up the outside staircase of her small, neat two-story home and directly into the dining room, it occurred to me that Señor Mezza intended for us to fill up our stomachs once again. Was this perhaps in preparation for what was yet to come on our journey?

There were three square, cloth-covered tables for four in the bright space. With windows on three of the white-washed walls and a stone fireplace on the fourth, the room took up the complete top floor of the house. Clearly, she had done this before. A small inside staircase led down presumably to the kitchen. One of the tables was set with a white table cloth adorned with three inches of what appeared to be hand-made lace. The plates were yellow, and the thick-walled glasses were red. The effect was quite startling.

Edward immediately pulled his enormous camera up to his face, and I was fully expecting Fabia to punch it to the floor. Instead, Edward, in very clear Spanish said, "*¿Puedo por favor tome una fotografía?*"

Fabia smiled demurely and struck a pose. Before Edward took the shot, he looked at us, shrugged, and then proceeded to photograph Fabia from all angles. She clearly loved it, but I was fairly certain that Edward had actually only wanted to photograph the dining room. Oh well, he seemed to have made a friend. And he had completely astonished me with his Spanish! Another hidden talent in our Edward, I was thinking.

All this time, Faith was examining the tablecloths, turning the lace over and over in her hand. She sidled up to me and whispered, "Do you think she made this herself?"

I shrugged while Faith sidled over to Edward and whispered in his ear, after which he asked Fabia a question, presumably about the provenance of the lace. Just then, Señor Mezza himself finally huffed to the top of the stairs and into the dining room. He then proceeded to give us instructions about where to sit and what we would eat.

"We will begin with our Fabia's famous ceviche which today is *corvina* marinated in a mixture of lemon and lime."

We must have looked puzzled.

Edward illuminated us. "*Corvina* is sea bass," he said knowledgeably, making a few notes in what looked to me like a blue-covered Moleskine notebook. Who knew he had Ernest Hemmingway proclivities?

Faith nodded thoughtfully. Señor Mezza continued while Fabia looked on. I was beginning to wonder just who was doing the food preparation.

"Yes," he said, "just so. Sea bass. You are quite right, Señor Edward." He was sort of smiling in Edward's direction. "Yes, where was I? Oh yes. Following the *Corvina*, we shall take Fabia's magnificent *Casado,* which she makes with sweet red peppers and onions. They will be sautéed with chicken and plantains and finished with fresh avocado, then served over rice." He looked most pleased with himself, and Fabia even smiled at him for the first time. Maybe she did understand English after all. My stomach growled in anticipation.

Faith seemed uncharacteristically quiet as we hungrily made our way through Fabia's magnificent lunch. Señor Mezza had not been joking.

Edward continued to flirt with Fabia, so much so that she allowed him to take photos of her work from all directions. I tried to listen to their conversation, but my Spanish was too rusty for me to depend reliably on my own translation. At one point, I thought Edward said he would take her home! She giggled at that and brought him a jar of her ceviche, which I had not known until that moment could be bottled. She placed it on the table and continued to rattle on in Spanish. It appeared she was telling Edward about the contents of the jar. He was nodding, smiling and asking questions. I turned to Faith, who was still quiet.

"Faith," I said, trying to break her away from what appeared to be a puzzling daydream. "Are you still with us?"

She grunted a bit, then seemed to shake herself. She smiled. "You know, Jenn, It's been a long time since I had the chance to be away from James to think about things."

"What kind of things?" I said, pouring myself another glass of the delicious *fresco* Fabio had made, allegedly using pineapple and mango mixed with milk, although I seemed to detect a bit of seasoning. Could it be rum? Whatever, it was yummy.

"Oh, you know, just...things." Faith took a sip of her own *fresco*. "Have you ever wondered if you're on the right path?"

I must have looked startled that she should even have to ask this question of someone who was clearly on some kind of a Quixotic journey into never-never land.

"Sorry," she said, "of course, you are probably the only person in the world who really does understand what I'm talking about."

"Is this about James...and you?"

"Partly, but that's not all of it. I haven't really figured out where my line of reasoning is taking me, but when I do, you'll be the first to know." She meditatively rubbed a piece of the tablecloth lace between her fingers, then smiled that perfect smile that took me back to our high school days when it would light up a room and melt the hearts of every boy in the vicinity. Bitch! But I loved her anyway.

Just then, Señor Mezza got up and said he was off to use the facilities. It was the ten-minute warning, and then we were all expected back in the van. We said our thank-yous to Fabia, who seemed to linger just a bit with Edward, holding his hand for just a moment too long. He smiled at her, and she disappeared downstairs only to emerge into the sunshine at the side of the van a few minutes later. She was holding a small box which she gave to Edward. He didn't seem a bit surprised. There was simple red lettering on the side of the box. It said:

FABIA'S COSITAS

...whatever that meant.

Dream Trips You Didn't See Coming

Of all the wonderful experiences people can have through travel, you'd think that the most visited tourist attractions would be the wonders of nature—the Grand Canyon, Angel Falls – or even historical wonders such as the Great Wall of China or the library at Ephesus. You'd think that, but you'd be wrong. No, according to recent statistics, the list of the world's most visited tourist attractions is headed by the strip in Las Vegas followed closely behind by Times Square in New York. And both Disneyland in California and Disney World in Florida made the top ten. What does that say about us as a species? I shudder to think, but I also shudder when I think that one of the places high on my list of places to see before I die is Las Vegas. Costa Rica made me seriously question that choice.

To be fair, I suppose it might be useful to define a tourist attraction. Perhaps natural wonders might be off the list, but you have to admit that the Great Wall is every bit as man-made as the Las Vegas strip, *n'est ce pas*? Anyway, we humans are a funny bunch.

We did finally make it to the Pacific coast. The distance from San José to Manuel Antonio Park is somewhere in the vicinity of 175 kilometres, and it's important to point out that there is a modern highway. Our route, though, as planned by Señor Mezza, took us over a shorter route as measured by mileage but vastly slower as measured by ruts, bridges, potholes and beauty. Although the tourist advisors online told me that the drive would take a mere three hours, it took more than five, not counting our lunch stop.

We finally pulled into tiny Quepos, the small, dusty, but bustling capital of the region of Puntarenas on the Pacific coast known as the gateway to Manuel Antonio Park. I had been told and had read that this park was not to be missed, but my primary interest in Puntarenas was that it was home to *Café Exquisito*. I was getting closer to the highlight of the trip, and my excitement was mounting. We were hot, tired, and seriously jostled but happy to have seen a bit of the Costa Rican countryside along the way. Oddly, Faith and Edward seemed to be bonding over camera equipment. Faith had been jabbering to him about cameras ever since she pulled a small specimen out of her suitcase. I had fallen asleep after one too many mentions of the acronym DSLR, whatever that meant. I was thinking that I ought to have known, but it was too much trouble to try to remember, so I drifted off. When I woke up, and I realized we had arrived in Quepos, I was mortified to have lost a half-hour of sightseeing out the window. *How in the world could I have fallen asleep when I was supposed to be so excited?*

Señor Mezza pulled the van into a parking spot outside a brightly coloured storefront and told us that he had a small errand to do before he took us to our hotel.

"Please," he said, handing us bottles of water from the cooler he kept in the back, "please feel free to walk around and stretch your legs. It is but a short drive to the hotel, but it has been a long drive to Quepos!" He smiled as he tapped a phone number into his cell phone and headed toward the building next door. He disappeared.

We all got out and dutifully stretched, trying to take in the sun that was now setting over the water. The town looked a bit dreamy, although I could see that it was slightly decaying. There is nothing like dusky light to bring out the best in everything. I certainly knew that I looked better at dusk than at high noon. Undoubtedly, today was a case in point.

Ten minutes later, Señor Mezza returned to the car, phone stowed once again in the upper left-hand pocket of his white cotton shirt. He was smiling and whistling. "Everything is prepared. We are ready to go."

And go we did. We drove through Quepos and out the other side, making our way toward the park, or so Edward, who was following the Google map, told us. Five or so kilometres later, we finally reached the end of what appeared to be a driveway – a long one that seemed to go up at a precipitous angle through a tangle of tropical trees. The van turned in and started the climb.

After several serious downshifts and skidding on loose gravel, the van finally made it to the top of the hill, and we were seriously rewarded. We emerged in the courtyard of a small hotel.

"*Bienvenido a La Casa Exquisito!*" he said, beaming as he ceremoniously opened doors for us. The three of us tumbled out onto the cobbled pavement.

Good lord, I thought as we walked through the double doors and into an exquisite lobby, *how many companies are so exquisite that they actually use it in their name?* I'd have to ask him tomorrow if there was any connection between this hotel and Dad's coffee source. Maybe they were all part of the same company.

We dropped our baggage at our feet—all three of us—all the better to gape, open-mouthed at the three-story-high ceiling resplendent with a wrought iron chandelier that looked like it had been plucked right out of a nineteenth-century hacienda owned by some coffee baron of yesteryear. Edward immediately whipped out his camera and began clicking madly. Oddly, so did Faith until she was drawn like a moth to a flame toward the three-story high draperies of finely fashioned lace. She caressed the lace for a brief second, then started to photograph it close up before returning to where I was standing in the middle of the foyer.

We looked around to find the sun-washed stucco walls covered in stunning artwork of a distinctly Central American flavour. The floors were of highly polished mahogany, and the front desk, festooned with more billowing mile-high drapes, seemed to be fashioned from iridescent marble. It was, in a word, exquisite. And you'd never have guessed from seeing it from the outside.

"It is nice, no?" Señor Mezza asked as he led us to the desk where it appeared we were already registered.

"It is nice, yes!" we said almost in unison.

The front desk clerk, a stunningly gorgeous young woman with masses of black hair and skin the colour of *café au lait,* came out from behind the desk to greet us. With her hand extended in greeting, she stepped down from the little step that raised the whole desk about a foot.

"You are very welcome..." she said as she stumbled on her mile-high stilettos directly into Edward's arms. He looked a bit stunned – as stunned as the rest of us felt.

"Oh dear," she said as she righted herself, pulling down her teeny-weeny mini skirt so that it once again covered her butt cheeks and not much else. "I am so clumsy."

She batted her eyes at Edward, and for the briefest of seconds, I thought that she had done it on purpose.

"Absolutely no problem," he said helping her to her feet, his eyes never leaving those long, shapely legs made all the more impressive because of the heels. Even the stiletto-loving interns at *Vivacity* would have been impressed. "I'm Edward, by the way," he said. The fact that he was able to recover so quickly in the face of what I supposed he considered to be massive embarrassment surprised me. Perhaps I didn't have as good a handle on Edward as I thought I did.

"And I am Valentina," she said when she had her bearings again. (Between us, I didn't think she had ever lost them – I'd have to discuss this with Faith later.) Oddly, her accent was British.

Faith looked at Edward, who was still staring at Valentina's legs and shook her head. Then she held out her hand to Valentina and introduced herself.

Valentina then turned to me. "And you must be Ms. Postman!" she said, almost gushing.

What in the world was that all about? I thought as I shook her hand, jingling her stack of bangles.

She then turned back to the desk where our room keys had already been laid out. It seemed that Faith and I wouldn't be sharing after all. We all had separate keys.

"My father will be along to have a cocktail with you in the Cave Bar at seven pm. You will find it on the lower level," Valentina said, handing us our individual keys. "Mr. Edward, you are in room 203 and Ms. Faith, you are in room 204." She looked back and forth between the two of them and smiled. "They are not connected, by the way."

I thought I saw a bit of a flush creep into Faith's smooth cheeks.

Then Valentina turned to me. "Ms. Postman, you are in 303, on the top floor. I do hope that you will all like your accommodations. If there is anything I can do?"

"Does your father own the hotel?" I asked.

She looked at me as if slightly puzzled for just the briefest of moments. "But, of course, Ms. Postman. Everyone knows that."

Evidently, I was not a part of that everyone, but I demurred to her and decided not to press for details until I had my bearings.

"Señor Murphy has owned this hotel for more than twenty years," Señor Mezza told us as he led us to the staircase with its black wrought-iron railing. He must have noticed my confusion.

Murphy? I thought. *How unusual. And why was Señor Mezza showing us to our rooms? Surely, they had staff to do that.* He certainly did seem to be "in" with everyone.

"Before I take you to your rooms," he said, "I would like to show you the swimming pool so that you might use it should you wish to do so during your stay."

We dutifully followed him, leaving our big luggage in the lobby, presumably so that some minion could take it on an elevator—at least, I supposed they had an elevator. At the first landing, he led us down a corridor and out a door into brilliant sunshine. We were momentarily blinded by the light dancing off the ripples in an extraordinary infinity pool. It was, however, what appeared beyond infinity that had me mesmerized. The hotel was indeed perched on the side of a small mountain that overlooked the Pacific. Below us, as far as the eye could see, stretched a powder-white beach almost devoid of beach-goers. I looked at the canopy of trees between us and the beach and wondered how we could get down to it—as soon as possible.

"That is *Playa Espadilla*," he said when he saw me gawking at the beach. "It leads into Manuel Antonio Park. The plantation is just inland," he said, pointing in the opposite direction.

At that moment, I didn't really care much about coffee, fruit or even Juan; I was trying to wrap my head around how my father had managed to swing this obviously expensive accommodation for the three of us. And just who was this Mr. Murphy whom we were all supposed to know about? I'd have to get out Mr. Google—that is, if they had Wi-Fi.

"Is there Wi-Fi here, Señor Mezza?" I said, turning from the view.

"But of course!" he said. "That is when there is power."

Well, that didn't sound so exquisite.

"Does the power go out often?" Faith said. She had already kicked off her shoes and was in the process of dipping a toe in the pool. Edward was photographing everything in sight as if it might disappear at any moment.

"Not often. About twice a week. But there is a generator for the kitchen."

Yikes, that seemed often to me, especially at such a fancy place.

"Let us proceed. You must all be longing for a bath. Right this way," he said, leading us back inside and up the stairs.

After Faith and Edward disappeared into their second-floor rooms (I could hear a bit of a gasp from Faith and wondered if she had seen a lizard since there did seem to be many around), Señor Mezza led me up to the top floor, where we stopped outside of a double set of what appeared to be massive mahogany doors.

"And here is your…room," he said with a flourish of a hand. "I will not be able to join you this evening when Señor Murphy meets you for a drink, but I will return tomorrow morning sharp at 10 am to take you to the plantation. I do wish you a wonderful evening. Should you wish anything at all, you will find a small panel inside the door to the right. It will be marked 'assistance,' and should you push it, someone will immediately appear at your door."

And with that, he disappeared down the stairs. I turned the large brass key in the lock and stepped inside.

I found myself in the open foyer of the most beautiful hotel suite my imagination could have created. Once again, I had to pick my jaw up off the floor. I dropped my carry-on bag onto what appeared to be an intricately inlaid marble floor. I was drawn immediately to the wall of floor-to-ceiling windows that opened onto an enormous wrap-around terrace with a view that was even more spectacular than the one from the swimming pool, owing no doubt to its greater height. I could see for miles along the beach and out to sea. *What in the world am I doing he*re? I wondered. *Does Dad know about this place?*

I immediately came to my senses, pulling my phone out of my purse and taking pictures as fast as I could. As I did, I heard the ping of my text messages. It was Faith.

"OMG. What does your room look like? Mine is incredible!!!"

"Incredible here, too." I texted back. Then, "Come up immediately." I had to share this with her.

Within seconds, Faith was at my door, giving me just enough time to notice that there was a bottle of champagne in an ice bucket on the marble-topped coffee table in front of the window. There were three cut-crystal champagne glasses arranged on a silver tray beside it.

I opened the door and led Faith out onto the terrace through the living room area. I hadn't even had time to look at the bedroom or bathroom (there turned out to be two—yes, two bathrooms!).

"How in the world..." Faith said as she was clearly speechless at the view, the room, the amenities, as was I.

"I don't know, Faith. I'm in a bit of a fog. I wonder if Dad knows where we're staying. His admin assistant made the arrangements, but I wonder if she might have gone overboard a bit. This hotel must be costing them a fortune. I'm going to be in so much trouble." I may have been thinking I'd be in a whole lot of trouble, but I wasn't having any trouble opening the champagne or picturing us here on the terrace, or in the pool, or in the hot tub for the next few days.

I expertly removed the cork with only a slight pop (Matt would have been proud) and poured two glasses of bubbly.

"Jenn, I never for a moment expected anything like this. What's going on? And who is Señor Murphy, and why are we having a drink with him tonight?" She grabbed the champagne flute from me and gulped in a very unladylike way, although it did occur to me that this was not the time for lady-likeness.

"I haven't the slightest idea," I said, bubbles tickling my nose as I sipped happily. I expected someone to walk in at any moment and say, "Surprise!" you're really staying at the hostel in Quepos. If that happened, I at least wanted to finish the champagne and have my photos to post on Facebook. I think I had a brief thought of making Andrew a bit crazy as he blogged around the world without his suit. "Have you seen Edward?" I said, coming back into the present, as dream-like as it was. "Is his room like this?"

"I'd guess that they're all like this," Faith said, walking around and into the bedroom. "I just can't figure out what we're doing here!" Then she shrieked. "My room is fantastic, but I don't have a separate bedroom with a two-person Jacuzzi in a bow window…or a spa for a bathroom!" She shrieked again. I ran into the other room.

"Oh. My. Actual. God." I said, covering my mouth with my free hand. "This is crazy!"

"Crazy wonderful," Faith said, holding out her glass for a refill.

She followed me back out to the living room and refilled both our glasses. We flopped into the cream-coloured, half-moon suede couch that faced the spectacular view and put our feet up on the coffee table – marble top be damned. "I suppose I'll have to call Dad later. I think I'll wait until later, though. I don't want the fantasy life to end quite yet."

So we finished the bottle of champagne while sitting on mattress-topped teak chaise longues on the terrace. With our faces turned toward the sun, we were feeling ever so relaxed when Faith sat up straight and said, "Is that my phone ringing?" It was.

She raced for the sliding door, almost tripping over the table between us toward the couch where she had laid it. I could hear her muffled voice from inside as I sat back and continued relaxing. A few minutes later, she returned, but her giggles had not.

"That was James."

"Checking up on you?" I drained my glass and set it down on the table. When I looked up at Faith, who was still standing in the open doorway, she wasn't smiling.

"In fact," she said, "he was." She flopped down on her chair and looked at her empty glass. "Anything stronger around here?"

"Come on, "I said, "it couldn't have been that bad."

"Well, he told me that I should get on a plane and come home. How bad does that sound to you?"

"We've only been gone for three days," I said, feeling offended for her. "Besides, he didn't stop you from coming. He was on board for a girls' getaway."

Faith sort of screwed up her mouth in a most unbecoming way.

"He was on board, wasn't he?"

"Not precisely," she said. "Okay, maybe he told me not to go." She screwed up her mouth again. "Well, he might have added, or else."

"Not to go? What is he? A refugee from the 1960s?" I was sitting up in full-on feminist indignation now. "Has he forgotten what century this is? And 'or else' what?"

"Welcome to my world," Faith said, trying to get another drop out of the bottom of her glass. "He really does think that I'd be happiest if I stayed at home and waited on him hand and foot, and he gave me wads of money to play with."

"You'd be happiest? I think he means he'd be happiest. Was he always like this?"

"Now that I look back, I think the signs were there," she said. "But I chose to interpret them as love and care. I guess I felt protected or something. Besides, I was still working full-time."

"What did you need to be protected from?" I was sitting up straight now, facing her. "I mean, when we were in high school, you were one of the only girls who I thought knew who she was. You didn't suffer fools gladly, that's for sure."

"You'd be surprised how insecure the captain of the cheerleading squad can be," she said, twisting a strand of that beautiful blonde hair of hers.

"Oh boy, Faith. I didn't know."

"Of course, you didn't! I wouldn't have had it any other way. Anyway, it's like my father told me that last time I was over there moaning about James. He said I hadn't made many mistakes in my life, but James was probably one of them."

"Wow. He really said that?"

"To be fair," she said slowly, "I had just told Mom and Dad that I thought I was going to get a divorce. So I guess if a father can't voice his true feelings at that point, I don't know when he can."

I was stunned. Divorced? Faith hadn't said a thing about this revelation. She saw my reaction.

"Sorry I didn't tell you, but this has been coming for a very long time. Since before you came back to Cork Harbour."

"I feel so foolish. I've been laying out my own problems at your feet for months, and here you've been suffering in silence."

"No need to get so dramatic about it," she said, going back inside to rummage through the mini-bar. "I haven't actually been suffering. I've been plotting." She returned in triumph with two mini bottles of some unremarkable sauvignon blanc, which she opened and poured into the two champagne flutes. She sat back down and put her feet up on the lounge again.

"What do you mean plotting?"

"Well, I've been researching my options, and when you said you wanted to come here to Costa Rica, I thought how perfect this was. I'd do some experiential research on being away from James—and maybe have a bit of fun without someone breathing down my neck." She looked toward the beach and swept her hand across the view. "And I do have to say that I didn't expect in my wildest dreams that it would be this incredible!" Finally, she smiled.

"It is pretty fantastic, isn't it?" I said, looking at my watch. "Oh god, it's getting late. We probably ought to primp up before meeting Señor Murphy."

Faith hiccupped loudly. "Yeah, Señor Murphy. What's that all about?"

I guess we were about to find out.

Does a New Life Really Begin at the End of Your Comfort Zone?

An hour later, as I made my way down the stairs toward the foyer, I could see Edward and Valentina below. I looked around, noting for the first time since we had arrived that although there didn't seem to be many other people around, there were at least two other guests in-house. At that moment, they were standing at the front desk, their matching Louis Vuitton luggage at their sides, having a lively conversation with the most beautiful "boy" I had ever seen. He was somewhere between twenty and thirty with dark hair and a chiselled jawline so sharp that I thought if I touched it, it might make at least a paper cut. He was smiling a kind of half-smile as the older couple chatted with him. When he glanced in my direction briefly, I felt a bit of a flutter. And it wasn't up as high as my chest, either. *Note to self*, I thought, *this one is dangerous.*

I was still standing on the first landing when my attention was drawn back to Edward and Valentina, who were still tête-à-tête on one of the velvet couches that flanked the enormous stone fireplace. It was clear to me that Valentina was off duty. She was flirting madly.

She was wearing some kind of filmy white dress with a plunging neckline. Her throat was adorned with what looked from a distance to be a huge crystal-embellished pendant on a black velvet cord. Her hair was swept over one shoulder where it bobbed fetchingly as she nodded her head at Edward's clearly witty remarks—I thought they must be witty since she was laughing. It was, however, difficult for me to believe that he was saying anything remotely humorous. It certainly wasn't in his nature — or at least the nature he had shown to date. But she was, indeed, laughing.

Before I could make my way over to break up the little giggle fest, Faith came bouncing down the stairs behind me.

"Hey, Jenn, what's going on?" She glanced toward Edward and Valentina, frowning. "What's she on about?"

"Let's go find out, shall we?" I said, linking my arm to hers.

They hardly noticed us, so engrossed they were in whatever they were finding so amusing. I coughed slightly. Valentina looked up.

"Ms. Postman, how delightful to see you." She smoothed her skirt unnecessarily as she stood up. "My father will join us in the Cave Bar in precisely eleven minutes. Shall we?" The chiffon-like folds of her skirt swayed as she walked toward the staircase leading down.

Clearly, we were not going to be let in on the joke she and Edward had been sharing.

Edward also stood up. "Jenn, I've been researching several fruit plantations in addition to the coffee plantations." He stooped down and picked up his tablet, which I hadn't noticed was on the table beside the couch. "Valentina has been very helpful." His eyes flickered momentarily toward Valentina, then Faith. "I've taken the liberty of telephoning Señor Mezza to tell him we'd like to take a more in-depth look at several places after our main visit to *Café Exquisito* if that's all right with you. Of course." He waited a moment for my slight nod of the head, the bobbing of which was involuntary, I must say, and then he continued. "Also, I thought that we might take advantage of the opportunity for a slightly more active visit. A bit of participant observation, if you will."

Participant observation? That was an expression I hadn't heard since I took an educational research methods course in grad school. I was starting to worry.

Valentina began making motions that we should follow her, or at least that's what I thought she was doing, but I had the feeling it was going to be a bit like herding cats.

"Do you think you could be a bit more specific? Exactly how much 'participation' did you have in mind?"

"Don't worry," he said, "it won't be anything you can't handle." He looked down at his tablet before continuing. "But you might want to wear some kind of hiking shoes."

Hiking shoes? This is not good, I thought. *What in the world has he gotten us into?*

Faith was still standing beside me, now with her arms crossed. "As thrilling as that sounds, I might have to beg off. I haven't really brought clothes for participant observation." She uncrossed her arms and leaned on the back of the nearby couch. None of us had yet moved to follow Valentina.

"Faith, you're not getting out of it that easily. I'll lend you something."

She sighed and shrugged, then turned to follow Valentina, who was nervously checking her watch. Given that she had mentioned precisely eleven minutes, I was getting the impression that her father was a bit of a punctuality Nazi.

Valentina led us down the stairs that wound underground from the lobby. The stairwell got darker and darker as we descended what appeared to be about two stories. The farther down we went, the creepier the lighting became. It started out being regular if expensive crystal sconces, but by the time we had reached about the halfway point, the wall sconces seemed to have given way to simple dots of bluish light that gave Valentina's dress an otherworldly hue and the rest of us a facial resemblance to a cadaver. It was a bit unnerving.

At the bottom of the stairwell, we found ourselves in a kind of lobby whose marble walls were illuminated by more dots of bluish light emanating from the ceiling. On the far wall was what appeared to be an arch-shaped wooden door replete with wrought iron hinges and a large knocker. Above the door hung a sign that said simply: *The Cave.* For the briefest of moments, I thought I caught sight of a bat but quickly realized my mind was playing tricks on me.

Valentina knocked three times (odd that she wasn't able to simply open the door, I thought at the time), after which the door mysteriously opened with a bit of a creak. We followed her through the archway into an extraordinary space that did, in fact, appear to be a real cave, but a cave that we lit by what seemed to be millions of tiny specks of light. Along the right-hand side was a bar that seemed to be floating off the ground because of the light that emanated from beneath it. The top was translucent, blush-coloured marble, on top of which were dozens of votive candles in cut-crystal spheres.

As we marvelled at this scene (even Edward was astonished enough to have forgotten to start taking photos), an attractive older man with graying temples (damn, why does that look so good on men but not so much on women?) and a smile that displayed a set of extraordinarily, even white teeth. His blue eyes seemed to dance in the candlelight. I thought I was in love. Turns out, however, that it was Valentina's father. And that wasn't all, but I didn't know it at the time.

When Señor Murphy spoke, I was momentarily caught off guard by his slight Irish lilt and his dazzling good looks. Very attractive people seemed to be the Costa Rican hallmark. I could hardly wait to continue my search for Juan, whom I had nearly forgotten in the unreality of our surroundings. I couldn't lose sight of why I was here, although finding him seemed a dimmer and even more fatuous chase now than it had when I first conned my father into footing the bill for this trip.

"I'm so glad you were able to finally make the trip, Jenn. I may call you Jenn?"

I nodded—he could have called me anything he wanted at that moment for all I cared. He continued.

"I must say I was a wee bit surprised when your father called me. Of course, I wasn't surprised that he called, only that you wanted to come."

"So…you know my father," I said when I finally found my tongue.

He looked at me directly in the face and then started to laugh. "Oh, you had me going for a moment there, but I should have expected that. Your dad was always having me on." He laughed, and everyone laughed. Except me. I hadn't the foggiest notion what he was talking about, but before I could ask, he was on to taking drink orders.

"You'll have a Guinness now, won't you, Edward?" Before Edward could answer, Señor Murphy—or whatever he was supposed to be called—beckoned to the bartender, a young man every bit as beautiful as the one currently at the front desk. *No, scratch that*, I thought, *it actually is that young man. How did he get down here without us seeing him?*

"You have all met my youngest son, Conor, I presume?"

Geesh, this really was an incestuous place – or maybe just an extremely well-run family business where everyone is involved.

"Wow, Señor Murphy," Faith said, sipping on the dirty martini that had magically appeared only moments after she expressed an interest in one, "your whole family must work here!"

"Yes, at the moment. Please, everyone calls me Murph. That Señor Murphy nonsense is to amuse the tourists. You three certainly aren't tourists."

But, yes, I wanted to say to him, we are tourists. Instead of saying anything, I took a sip of my own very delicious Manhattan that had also magically appeared. I was so confused – and getting more uncomfortable by the minute.

Murph raised his glass. "A toast to begin the evening."

We dutifully raised our glasses, including both Valentina and Conor, who were drinking Guinness, too.

"May you have the hindsight to know where you've been, the foresight to know where you're going, and the insight to know when you've gone too far." Then he winked – at me.

It was quite a sentiment—of Irish provenance, I had no doubt—and one that I thought I'd have to remember for the rest of this trip. *Whatever kind of conversation was I going to have with my father later?* I wondered.

After the toasting, Faith asked Murph about *The Cave*. He told us that it *was* an actual cave sculpted out of the hill on which the hotel was built. They had found it during the renovation process and decided that it would be the perfect bar. Evidently, the ritual of knocking on the door was also to amuse the tourists. There was a fairly pedestrian entrance at the other end of the bar, which led to the restrooms and onto the dining room, but entering that way was far less entertaining, according to our friendly proprietors. That must have been the route Conor had taken to beat us to the bar.

"You could have told me about your family's connection," Faith said, sliding onto the barstool beside me sometime later.

I just shook my head in bewilderment. "What on earth are you talking about?

"Stop playing coy. It's me you're talking to here, Jenn." She hiccupped amiably.

"Really, Faith, I have no idea what's going on."

"I just had a little conversation with the delicious Conor over there." She looked over at him with what I could only interpret with lust in her eyes. I thought I heard a slight sigh. "By the way, you might as well send Matt a message to come on down. He'd be more Conor's type than I am."

"Married women not his type?" I know that sounded catty, but I hadn't meant for it to come out that way. If Faith noticed, she didn't say anything.

"Not just *married* women. *All* women. But I'll get over it. Anyway, back to our conversation. If you truly are in the dark, you're in for quite a surprise, I'd say."

I was starting to get exasperated with everyone. If there was some kind of secret, some news, some revelation I wasn't in on, I needed to be. I threatened Faith with a swift return to Cork Harbour, so she spilled.

"According to the delicious Conor, your father and Murph are business partners."

I must have looked as lost as I felt.

"It explains a lot, you know." She ate the last of her three olives from her dirty martini expertly prepared for her by Conor. "Now I know why your father was so quick to say yes to this little junket." She stopped and looked at me again, presumably for any sign of prior knowledge on my part. "Jenn, your father is a part-owner of this hotel."

You could have knocked me over with a feather, as the saying goes, only this time it was really true. I very nearly fell off the barstool. I looked over at Murph, who actually had Edward laughing about something. This situation was impossible—and not just the laughing Edward part. How could my father be the part-owner of a hotel in Costa Rica, of all places and his family not know about it? Scratch that—and me not know about it? I had no doubt whatsoever that Mom knew since they told each other everything. Or so I thought, anyway. But how could he have let us come down here and not have told us this? Perhaps even more intriguing than 'how' was the question of 'why.'

I looked around for my phone and realized that I'd left it upstairs. Any contact with Dad would have to wait.

Faith was truly shocked to find out that even I didn't know about this connection. She suggested that I try to get a few minutes relatively alone with our host to find out more. That was easier said than done. Murph was a truly entertaining host who clearly loved being the centre of attention. Valentina was a close second. So, I didn't have much of a chance of getting the details of this little secret any time soon. This became even a dimmer possibility when Mrs. Señor Murphy arrived.

Paloma Murphy made a grand entrance through *The Cave* doors at precisely eight p.m. It was as if the rest of the family had been set upon us earlier to warm us up. I suppose you can never be quite ready for Paloma, but we didn't know it then.

Señora Murphy entered, and the atmosphere was never the same again. Even though, at that precise moment, neither Faith nor I nor Edward knew who she was, there was a palpable change in the air. It was suddenly electrified—she, herself, exuded equal parts eccentricity and elegance. The three of us stopped our conversations in their tracks and were immediately transfixed by her presence. Even Murph stopped—for the briefest of moments—the story that he was relating to Edward and two other men who had wandered into our little party and whom I had yet to meet. *Where have I seen her before?* I wondered.

Valentina looked in her mother's direction, shrugged and went back to her martini—her third by my rather unreliable count. Before Murph could even introduce her all around, Paloma made a bee-line for me. Me.

The voice was husky as if she had inhaled one or two too many cigarettes in her day and perhaps downed a whiskey or two in a rush. "Jennifer Postman," she said, extending both arms, the better to grip me in an unwelcome embrace. "I finally meet you!" The arms full of bangles (even more than Valentina sported) and dripping with purple chiffon embraced me to her rather ample bosom. "I am Paloma." If her bosom was ample, the rest of her was skin and bones.

Then it struck me. It was Lauren Bacall! Well, it was the actress who had played her in a recent film. The shoulder-length blonde hair in a 1950's Pageboy, the full, red lips, the slight scent of tobacco mixed with mouthwash. It was Paloma Belmonte, actress and former high fashion model. Close up, it was clear that she was a well-preserved sixty without apparent benefit of plastic surgery. The breasts, of course, were another matter altogether. But wait, why did she seem to think she knew me?

"I have waited so very long to finally meet you. Your father, he tells me much about you."

At this, Murph scowled just a bit. "My darling, Jenn doesn't even know you yet."

"Oh, but she will. We have much to catch up on." She turned to Conor, who was lounging at the end of the bar with the two men who had joined the group. "Conor, darling, pour Mummy a Jameson. I will take it neat, and I will have it at my table." She turned to Murph. "And you, my dear husband, will leave the women to their chatter."

She took me by the arm, giving me no choice but to be a good guest and go with her. I grabbed my drink on the way to the corner table with the black velvet banquette. As I left, I turned to Faith, who very clearly mouthed, "W.T.F.?"

When we were comfortably seated at her table (well, I was comfortable physically, but psychologically, it was a different story), formal introductions began. She introduced herself to me as Paloma Belmonte Murphy, model, actress and former lover of one Jackson Postman. My father. Neither she nor Murph nor either of her children, all of whom could hear every word, seemed the slightest bit concerned about this. Faith and Edward, however, appeared to be a different story. They were visibly leaning in our direction, trying to eavesdrop. If Paloma noticed, she didn't let on. I scowled at them as discreetly as I could.

Then Paloma began to pump me for current information about Jackson (no one on the planet called my father Jackson – he was Jack Postman to everyone except apparently former lovers). I updated her, and then it was my turn. I would not be put off any longer. I needed to know precisely what was going on. She, with a bit of help from Murph, who had now snuggled in beside his wife at the table, told me the whole story. At least, I thought it was the whole story.

Apparently, she and my father met when he was on a gap year just before he started graduate school. He and my mother had broken up when she went off to Paris to hone her French and study art with some artist whose name was unfamiliar to me. Mom had told me about that year. In fact, I always remembered that kind of faraway look she got when she talked about it. She had told me she wanted to be free for that year and told Dad to go off and have an adventure. If they were still in love at the end of their explorations, they would be married. And so they were. However, it had always seemed to me that, judging from her reaction when she remembered that year, Mom's adventure had taken something of a romantic turn. According to Paloma, Dad's did as well.

"I have only one photo of that interlude," Paloma said. "We were not like the young people of today. We chose to live our lives rather than record them constantly on telephones. We chose to keep our secrets to ourselves rather than broadcasting them to the world on our Facebook accounts. It was more delicious then."

Amen to that, I was thinking. Oh, for the good old days when privacy meant something and people cherished it.

Paloma glanced at Valentina, who was paying no attention whatsoever to her mother; rather, she was gazing lovingly at her cell phone screen. Paloma continued her story.

"You know," she said, finishing her Irish whiskey and motioning to Conor to refill her glass, "I have met your wonderful mother. She and your father attended our wedding, you know. In fact, I have one of her paintings in my bedroom. It is a beautiful watercolour of a Nova Scotian lighthouse. I will show it to you." Her slight Spanish accent was charming, but I wondered where it had gone when she played Lauren Bacall.

The whole story was a complete surprise to me. She and Dad had met in New York, where she was beginning to gain some traction as a model. They had kept company, as she put it, for three months, after which he told her he would be returning to the love of his life when he started business school in the fall. She was evidently fine with that, and they vowed to stay friends. They had been true to their vow. That fall, she was off to Paris for the spring shows and to become one of those 1970s super-models.

When Dad started his MBA that fall, Mom returned from her own Parisian sojourn to be with him, and they were married shortly after. It turned out that Murph was an old friend of Dad's from his undergraduate years who, as it happened, was by then a year ahead of Dad in the MBA program. Dad had been their matchmaker, and the rest was history. Well, at least in part. The business relationship was yet another story.

Paloma insisted that we needed to eat before there could be any further story-telling, so the business end of it would have to wait. She led the way upstairs to the dining room that had been laid out as if for a feast with honoured guests. I think that those guests were us.

"What in the world is she talking about?" Faith whispered as we went up the stairs.

"Not sure yet," I said, "but I intend to find out."

"She's really something, isn't she?" Faith said.

"Paloma? I guess." I was still somewhat confused.

When we reached the dining room, we all took our seats as indicated by place cards that looked like hand-done calligraphy. Faith was examining hers very closely as she sat down beside Valentina.

If we had been expecting authentic Costa Rican fare, we were going to be sorely disappointed because Paloma and Murph's chef was Parisian and had outdone herself on the French menu. We began with escargots *bourguignonne au parfum d'anis* (snails flambéed with licorice-flavoured Pernod, finished with a butter and garlic sauce), followed by *l'entrecôte sauce bordelaise avec portobello* (grilled striploin with red wine sauce and portobello mushrooms). Dessert was a triumph: perfect pavlova filled with Costa Rican fruits that had been preserved in syrup. Edward was in heaven. And Paloma forbade us to talk business while we ate. It seemed that eating was a bit of a religion to her, although you'd never know it to see her sinewy limbs.

By the time we were onto sipping our after-dinner port, Murph raised his glass once again to toast us. "And now," he said as he placed his glass back on the table, "I think we owe Jenn an explanation since her dear father seems to have kept her in the dark." He looked around as if to ensure that he had a rapt audience and then continued. "First, before we get to the business part of this story, you're probably wondering how it came to be that one of your father's old lovers," (the very thought made me cringe), "came to be married to one of his old grad school friends."

I do have to admit that this was precisely what I was wondering—that was after wondering about how it was that my father seemed to be in business with this unknown group, and he had somehow and for some reason kept it a secret from me.

"Indeed, it was quite a coincidence. Paloma was in Dublin for a photoshoot, and her group wandered into my pub one evening. We got to talking and found out that we had a mutual acquaintance. Well," he looked at Paloma, "it was love at first sight on my part. When we decided to marry, your father was at the top of the list. He tells the story a bit differently, I'll wager. He has always considered himself the matchmaker. He says he sent her to the pub!" He laughed.

"Did you live in Ireland after you were married?" Edward asked from his end of the table. I was a bit surprised that Edward didn't know all of this; he prided himself in being Dad's right-hand man.

"For a short while," Paloma said. "My work, however, did keep me on the move. We also had a home in Paris, but I was homesick the whole time."

"Ten years ago, Paloma and I decided to come back to Costa Rica," Murph said, taking up the story.

I was all ears. Paloma had already told me she was a born and at least partially bred tica (native Costa Rican) whose family lived in a large hacienda on a hill on the outskirts of San José. Her provenance was quite cosmopolitan in my view: her father was a businessman, and her mother had been something of a cultural philanthropist. She also told me that she had been 'discovered' as she put it one evening at the opera by a visiting model's agent from New York. (She suggested that I visit the National Theatre in San José: evidently, it was modelled on the Paris Opera House.) Beyond this impressive CV, I was still quite baffled by this whole situation.

"We wanted to find a business we would enjoy since Paloma thought she was retiring—although, as you all know, she couldn't keep herself out of the public eye and did one recent movie."

Paloma preened at this.

"We decided to search for an establishment to operate. Back in Dublin, I owned a pub. Did I tell you that?"

I had figured that when he had mentioned she walked into 'his' pub one evening, he wasn't just the bartender.

At this, Valentina raised her eyes from her cell phone, where they continued to be glued, her fingers tapping fairly constantly through dinner, much to her mother's obvious chagrin. Then the eyes rolled. "Oh please, Dad. He was like the proprietor of a string of high-end pubs and restaurants."

I was impressed. I guess that expensive MBA had been as valuable to him as I always thought it had been to my father.

He looked at Valentina and smiled. "My pretty daughter is right, as usual. They were reasonably successful, too, if you don't mind me saying. Made a wee bit of money when I sold on." He looked around at the room and at us. "When we came upon this old one, we were smitten. Set about figuring out how to get it up and running."

I was even more confused at this stage if that were possible. I sort of understood the connection between Murp and my dad — and Dad and Paloma — but I still didn't see how he could possibly be some kind of business partner here. In Costa Rica. All of this seemed so far away from him and his life in Cork Harbour at *Savoreaux*.

"And so I'm coming to the good part, Jenn, my girl. About your father." He took another sip of his almost-empty port glass and looked at me. "Bet you didn't know that your dad and I were in business school together."

Well, I did know, but only because just an hour or two earlier, his lovely wife had spilled the beans. But I let him continue.

"Well, we were. I was a year ahead, though I know I don't look any older." He smiled widely and flexed a muscle. "We kept in touch through the years, and when your dad moved out of the city and back to Cork Harbour, he invited me along to see the new business. He was several years in when I finally got away to visit him." He looked at me. "You were already long gone to make your fortune, Jenn, so I had not the pleasure of meeting you then. I did love that beautiful mother of yours, though."

"No more so than I did," Paloma said. "That's when he bought me that piece of her work I told you about, Jenn."

"So," I said, trying to figure things out, "Dad is somehow involved here?"

Murph laughed. "You could say that, love. He and I are equal partners on some business ventures here about. This is one of them." He gestured to one of his staff for more port. "I must say I was delighted when he called to tell me that you were coming on something of a marketing junket. Naturally, I freed up the suites for the three of you. You're like family to us. And he never did tell you, did he?" He chuckled a bit.

That much was undoubtedly clear to everyone. For some reason, Dad decided to spring this on us as a kind of surprise, and it seemed that Murph knew that. I looked over at Faith to see how she was reacting to all this news but saw that she was deep in conversation with Paloma, their two heads, one very dark and wild, the other blonde and sleek, intimately close. I wondered what they were discussing.

Why the 'Active' Vacation Might Not Live up to its Press

W hen Thoreau wrote, *"The man who goes alone can start today; but he who travels with another must wait till that other is ready,"* he must have been thinking about poor Edward.

When I made my way down the stairs to the lobby the following day, Edward was already there, waiting impatiently. I could tell that he was impatient because he was fiddling with the settings on his camera. I had observed that he fiddled when he was impatient.

I said good morning, poured myself a coffee from the urn on an ornate sideboard that was set out all morning for guests to help themselves and considered one of the tempting pastries on offer.

"Where's Faith?" I said as I bit into a flaky French-style *pain-au-chocolat. The Parisian chef must also have French pastry-chef-like talents*, I was thinking. It was divine.

"She just left."

"Hmm?" My mouth was full.

"In a car," he said. "Nice one, too."

How in the world could Faith have left in a car? How could Faith have left at all without telling me? It was so not like her.

"I got a text from her. Did you check your messages this morning?" Edward said

I had not. I quickly placed (jammed) the rest of the pastry in my mouth, wiped my hands on a tiny, starched linen napkin, and then fished my phone out of my tote bag. Yup. I had neglected to check my messages. And I had not yet called Dad. I wasn't ready for that conversation yet.

"Sorry to miss today's outing," it read. "need to follow up on an opportunity with Paloma. Talk later."

With Paloma? What in the world was this all about? At least, that might explain the fact that the car that picked her up was what Edward had referred to as a nice one. Good heavens, now I'd have to spend the day alone with Edward doing some kind of 'participant-observation' thingie. I was all in favour of the observing part – but the participating part? Not so much. My curiosity about what Faith might be up to would have to be put on the back burner for a while since Señor Mezza had just walked into the lobby and was gesturing us toward the waiting van.

The concept of the active vacation had somehow eluded me. My interests ran to loafing on the beach, reading schlocky books, and drinking margaritas by the gallon. Other people could run and jump and climb and generally exhaust themselves, but that wasn't my style. The fact that I wasn't technically on a vacation didn't change my perspective, which became increasingly entrenched as Edward regaled me with the joys of participation. Much to my increasing horror, what we were evidently going to participate in was picking coffee beans.

At first, I thought, *well, how bad can it be?* That was until he began to provide me with a few more details. As we made our way through beautiful roads flanked by wildly tangled foliage that created green knots of shade, Edward offered me detailed commentary on what we were about to experience. I rather thought I'd prefer just to be kept blissfully ignorant until the final destination. I'd deal with it then.

"Jenn, you do know, of course, that the best coffee is hand-picked rather than machine-picked, don't you?"

"What? Yes, I suppose it would be." I had put aside my ruminations about my father, Murph, Paloma and the lot of them and had been daydreaming about meeting Juan. I was wondering about who he really was and fantasizing just a little bit about who I'd like him to be. I knew very well that these two Juans might be very different species from one another. In fact, it was very probable that they were very unlike one another. But a girl can dream, can't she?

My fantasy Juan was tall, dark, very chiselled, brooding and waiting for me. How did he know I would be coming? Well, of course, he just knew. Remember, I used to work for a women's magazine. Despite second-wave feminism, the fantasy lives on in the pages of romance novels and magazine features.

Edward interrupted my reverie again. "Jenn, did you hear what I said?"

"Sorry, Edward, I was just thinking about something. What did you say?"

"I said that we were actually going to learn to pick coffee. I've slotted in three hours of hand-picking before we learn about the next steps in the process. I'm hoping to be able to get some great photos while we work. You probably won't need to take notes. You'll be able to recapture it later."

Whatever. Good lord. It was steaming hot outside the rarefied atmosphere of the air-conditioned van. Did he really think that I'd last three hours outdoors working on a coffee plantation? Then I thought, what if Juan is there? The plantation was owned by *Café Exquisito*, wasn't it? Then, it occurred to me that the note had been among the coffee packed for export, so it was highly unlikely that he was anywhere near the actual fields. That was unless they rotated or something. I had no idea. Oh well, I'd just have to keep waiting.

When we arrived at the plantation, we were greeted by a kind of welcome party. We were introduced to a variety of foremen and workers, so I made a note of their names and chatted with them briefly before we were handed our plastic baskets, which we were to sling over our shoulders like a giant cross-body hobo bag as if it were the 'it' bag of the season. Edward snapped a few photos, and then we were off to our destination: the coffee shrubs/trees, where we were instructed to look for the so-called cherries that were a deep, bright red and to leave the others that were not yet ripe enough. Before we began, Diego, the foremanin-charge, who was extremely deferential to me, I noticed, picked a ripe cherry from the tree to show us. Then he rolled it around in his hand and opened it up to reveal the two coffee beans inside. They weren't the deep, dark brown colour that I was accustomed to, but these *did* look like the coffee beans that I knew. Now we were talking.

As we picked, Diego told us about coffee harvesting, but the only thing I remember specifically was him saying that it took 100 kilos of coffee cherries to make 15 kilos of export-ready coffee. As I began to sweat and my fingers began to tingle from the effort, I was horrified at the amount of work involved. My respect for my daily cups of coffee was intensifying by the moment. Maybe Edward really was on the right track with all his veneration for our food and its sources.

"Hey, Juan Val Dez!" Diego shouted.

My neck snapped up from my labour, and I peered in the direction toward which he was calling. He was gesturing to an older man with what looked like an enormous straw bowl strapped to his waist. He waved a leathered hand and smiled at us from beneath his tattered straw sun hat. He was missing a tooth.

"Diego," I said, "is that Juan Val Dez?"

Diego laughed. "That's what we all call him. He reminds us of the guy in the advertisements. You know the ones?"

I did know them. Yes, Juan Val Dez was a fictitious coffee picker, and I knew that. Intellectually.

"What's his real name?"

"Oh, he *is* Juan." He turned and gestured toward a group of three pickers. "So are two of them. They come here from Nicaragua to work with us. They like us because we treat them better than the other plantations, of course." He seemed very proud of this. I couldn't blame him.

Oh, dear. This was going to be painful because I was beginning to think that I had better focus on the actual reason I told my father I wanted to come to Costa Rica. The whole Juan Val Dez thing was beginning to cloud my brain. So, I turned my attention to the coffee cherry picking despite what it was doing to my manicure. Eleanor would have been horrified!

True to his word, Edward kept us coffee picking for exactly three hours. When I looked at my paltry haul compared with the professional coffee pickers, my admiration for them and the eventual cup of coffee I might drink increased immeasurably.

After the participant observation of the coffee picking part, it seemed that we were to simply be observers of the next steps, where we learned about how they examined the coffee cherries, then passed them through a pulping machine where the skin and pulp were removed from the cherries to leave only the beans which then fermented in large tanks for 24 to 36 hours. Then, of course, they had to be dried and hulled to smooth perfection before they became what is known as green coffee—the stage they are in when the roasting process begins. It seemed that *Café Exquisito* exported green coffee beans to places that boasted on-site roasting (I'd seen a few of those boutique coffee places in Toronto) as well as the roasted ones that I had been unpacking when I found Juan's note.

By the time we had reached the point of knowing all about green coffee and observing the warehouse where the coffee was stored in large sacks, I was beyond exhausted. I surreptitiously pulled out my phone to check the time, ensuring that Edward didn't see me. He had convinced me early in the day that checking phones at any time throughout our experience would have seemed rude. I thought that he just didn't want to hear any beeps or pings interrupting his enjoyment of the fruits and things. However, I had complied and turned off the sounds. When I glanced at it in my tote bag, I was surprised to see that it was past five p.m.; I was less surprised to see that I had six text messages. They would have to wait until the drive home—if I could get any service.

Señor Mezza was just pulling the van up to the front of the warehouse as Edward and I profusely thanked Diego and his workers for a most informative day. Tomorrow we would visit the main hacienda of the plantation and experience a coffee

140

tasting. We were also going to meet the president and CEO of the company. I was looking forward to that—very much.

Coffee: The Most Important Meal of the Day

D id you know that people have been drinking coffee since the tenth century and that it probably originated in Ethiopia? Well, don't feel bad if you didn't know that; I was utterly oblivious to the history of my favourite drink (after wine) until the drive back to *Casa Exquisito,* during which Edward availed himself of the reading material that Diego had pressed into his willing hands just before we left. His monologue and the materials were designed to provide me with background information for the content I was supposed to be creating for Dad's customers, as well as to prepare us for tomorrow's coffee tasting. So I half-listened as I scrolled through the various text messages I had downloaded before we left the plantation.

There was a text from Mom asking how things were going. Then, one from Dad asked me to bring back a bag of the new *Café Exquisito* blend so he could test it before a wholesale purchase. There was one from Matt who was celebrating a big litigation win that might be auguring (I kid you not, he used that word) a promotion to partner. It ended, "Toronto still misses you!" There may also have been a crying emoji or two. That would be the first one I would answer as soon as I had cell service again. Then, buried down the list was one from my old boss, Eleanor, that I couldn't make heads or tails of. Something about me meeting with her or something. She seemed exercised by some kind of idea. Maybe Matt's text wouldn't be my priority after all. Just then, I noticed that I had service, so I quickly texted Eleanor back that I was out of the country (don't you just get a little thrill when you're able to say that to someone?) and would call when I returned. But there was nothing from Faith. What in the world was that woman up to?

"Are you sure Faith didn't mention where she was going today when you saw her leaving the hotel this morning?" I said, looking up from my phone.

"Jenn, we were talking about coffee. Have you heard a single thing I said?"

I'm sure I pouted just a little. "Of course. And I do appreciate it." I glanced at my phone again, lest I had missed something crucial while I had service. "It's just not like Faith to go off like that. Especially in a foreign country."

"Are you worried about your friend, Ms. Postman?" Señor Mezza interjected from the front seat. "If so, I can make a phone call. One call is all it will take. We will find her in but a moment." He glanced at me in the rearview mirror. "We have friends."

Something about how he said it suggested to me that I was to believe him—no doubt he and whomever else was part of the royal 'we' *did* have friends.

"Thank you, but I'm sure she's quite fine." I hoped I hadn't opened a can of worms here.

"Jenn, she was with Paloma. I'm sure she just had something that had to be done."

I sighed. I really didn't think that there was anything at all to worry about. I was just miffed about the mystery.

When we finally stumbled out of the van and into the hotel lobby, I felt so grubby that all I wanted to do was submerge myself in that delicious jetted tub in my suite, but before I did, I knocked on Faith's door. No answer. I really would have to wait now.

When I finally emerged from the tub and the general fluff-up I needed, the power had gone off. It's true. We had been warned about this possibility. Since the sun had set already, I had to break out the flashlight on my cell phone to finish dressing for dinner. After stubbing my toe twice on the frame of the four-poster bed and causing my carry-on bag to fall on my head from the shelf in the closet, I was ready to emerge.

I felt my way down the stairs in the gloom, hoping not to disgrace myself by falling. When I arrived in the lobby, everyone was already there holding glasses of champagne in the flickering light of what seemed like hundreds of candles. Paloma was resplendent in a filmy white dress edged by a fluttery, feather-like braid wound with what looked like filaments of gold. She was beaming as she handed me a glass.

"Jenn, my dear, you are here! I do hope your day was as charming as was ours!"

I wasn't at all sure I would have described my day as charming, but it was clear that she and Faith had enjoyed theirs. *Where is Faith, anyway?* I was thinking. I was soon to have my answer.

I had just begun an entertaining conversation with our genial host about his experiences with eccentric guests at properties such as his when Faith floated down the stairs – and it really did look like she was floating.

Her dress, equally as filmy and fluttery as Paloma's, drifted out behind her in cream-coloured waves that were back-lit by the candles on the floor of the first landing. Even her hair had the same ethereal quality, hanging in long, loose waves bouncing down past her shoulders. I was momentarily speechless. I had never in all my life seen Faith look as spectacular. What in the world had she and Paloma been up to today? A spa day? And why wasn't I invited? I looked down at my destroyed cuticles and pouted yet again.

Faith made a bee-line directly toward me, tripping over the leg of a chair in the semi-darkness as she did so, therefore restoring my view of her as my wonderfully down-to-earth BFF.

"Jenn, I have so much to tell you," she whispered in my ear, all the while beaming from ear to ear and pushing me away from Murph, who was beaming at Faith himself.

"You sure do," I said. "What in the world is going on?"

Faith picked up a champagne flute from the silver tray surrounded by twenty or thirty twinkling votives, then pushed me in the direction of the back patio where tables had been set up for dinner under the moonlight. The sound of the kitchen generator could be heard gently humming in the background.

"Okay, Faith. Spill. What have you been up to today? By the way, you look stunning."

"I do, don't I?"

Well, that wasn't like my modest friend. Something was up. "Faith?"

"Okay, okay," she said, leading me toward one of the tables. She pulled two chairs out from the table and practically pushed me into the one opposite her. "I am so excited."

"Clearly," I said wryly.

"Jenn, I think I've found my future direction." I must have looked very confused, a state in which I seemed to be continually finding myself since arriving in this country. "Okay, well, you remember those lace tablecloths that I was admiring at Fabia's?"

I had no idea what she was talking about. She continued.

"At that place Señor Mezza took us to lunch."

Then I remembered. Faith had been captivated by the lace trim on the tablecloths and had wondered about its provenance.

"Anyway, I happened to mention my admiration for this kind of hand-worked lace to Paloma last night when we were chatting, and she told me about her friend in Quepos who owned a boutique."

"A boutique in Quepos?" I found it hard to imagine that Quepos held any kind of 'boutique' that would be of interest to Faith, much less to a worldly jet-setter like Paloma.

"I know it sounds weird, but there really is a boutique owned by an ex-pat Quebecois fashion designer. She lives in a villa somewhere in these hills. I met her at the shop."

Faith's excitement reminded me of the little kids approaching the tea cup ride at Disney World a few years back.

When the entire story finally emerged, it seemed that Paloma's friend Babbette Gagné was indeed an ex-pat Quebecois whose evolution as a fashion designer had taken her from drapey, sarong-like dresses that could be worn six ways (OMG! Her!) to real dresses and a Costa Rica home base. It seemed that her real love was hand-worked lace with a particular emphasis on couture cocktail dresses, evening attire and wedding gowns. And so it turned out that both Faith and Paloma were wearing original Babbette Gagné dresses that evening.

Babbette had met an American banker who had been working in Montreal, fallen in love, married and moved to New York, which she absolutely hated. When the two of them had amassed enough money, they left NYC for Costa Rica, where she had set up her dream business – an online couture shop that sold one-of-a-kind dresses and gowns with the lace hand-worked by Costa Rican artisans.

"Didn't you write a piece in *Vivacity* about her once?"

"It does seem to ring a bell." I had no idea why I was being so coy. "Yes, I sort of did. The article was more about one of her designs. Her focus seems to have changed," I said, looking more closely at the exquisite dress that Faith wore so well. "So, how does all this relate to your new direction?"

"I'm going into business with Babbette and Paloma!"

After I picked my jaw up off the floor, Faith went on to explain that they had begun talking about expanding the online business to encompass a wider variety of designers and clothing lines. By the time she had finished, even I was convinced that she just might be able to pull it off. It did seem to be more up her alley than nursing ever was, in my view.

"What's James going to think?"

A bit of a cloud seemed to roll over Faith's beautiful face. "It won't matter," she said. "That's the other part of the decision that I've made. I'm leaving him. For sure. No turning back."

"Oh, Faith," I said, reaching out to hug her. "That's a huge decision. Are you ready to make it? I mean, being away might have clouded your thoughts."

She sat up straight. "Jenn, being away was what I needed for some breathing space to figure it all out. The truth is that this

146

decision has been coming for a year now. I was just trying to find the courage to take some action. I've made my decision, and I have to thank you for getting me away to a new experience. It's made all the difference." She took a deep breath. "Now I just have to tell James."

Faith knew that she had a rocky road ahead of her but that I'd be there for her. It was scary and exciting, and I was so happy for her. Now, if I could just find my own way forward—maybe supporting her and her decisions would be good for me, too.

The dinner gong sounded, and everyone began filing into the dining room and out onto its patio. Three hours later, we all filed out again, slept like corpses and awoke to a beautiful Costa Rican morning with the smell of fresh coffee wafting into our nostrils. Today was the day for the real coffee tasting. After another delicious Parisian breakfast courtesy of the inn's French chef, we were ready for a new adventure.

The coffee plantation's hacienda was situated on a gentle slope of astonishingly green grass just above the acres and acres of coffee. It was an impressive ochre-coloured Spanish-colonial style edifice with a large portico-like structure where our van stopped to let us out—Faith included today. We were ushered by a uniformed butler (yes, a butler!) through the round entry foyer that soared three floors above with an enormous cast-iron chandelier like the one in the hotel foyer above. We padded along over what appeared to be hand-painted marble tiles beneath our feet. The butler led us through to the back of the villa, where the coffee tasting room was located. We were to have a private tasting with *Café Exquisito*'s CEO and his tasting staff.

When we walked into the room, we were faced with a wall of floor-to-ceiling windows that looked out onto the acreage in the back—coffee trees as far as the eye could see. It was impressive—and so was the wonderful aroma of the coffee that they were preparing for us.

The floors in this room were a highly polished reddish wood as were the tables and chairs. The effect was one of warmth and comfort. Maybe if you drank as much coffee as the tasting staff, you needed to be surrounded by so much calmness!

Three insanely good-looking young men toiled behind the barista bar. They all looked up and smiled at us, displaying three uniformly beautiful sets of very white teeth. I made a mental note to ask them what kind of tooth whitener they used. Surely, drinking so much coffee would create havoc with that colour! After smiling and nodding in our direction, they all went back to work.

The butler suggested we make ourselves comfortable, and the 'boss' would be arriving presently.

Edward wandered over to pick up several slickly designed brochure booklets while Faith, camera in hand, stood by the windows snapping photos. I spent my time gazing at the baristas' backs and wondering if I'd ever find the real Juan Val Dez—or at least the one who really wrote that note. I sighed deeply enough that Edward looked up from his reading.

"Jenn? Everything okay?"

His concern was touching—it did seem sincere.

"Of course. Thanks for asking," I said. Then I changed the subject. "What's supposed to happen today? Do we just get ourselves a cup of coffee?"

"Uh-uh," he said, shaking his head and pointing to the glossy, colourful brochure. "We're going to have a real tasting like they do at wineries."

I think I snickered a little bit. I'd have to take really good notes, so I'd be able to relay all of the clearly impending hilarity to Matt. He always loved a good wine tasting, so I figured he'd find the idea of a coffee tasting in the same vein to be laughable at best. Just then, the butler returned.

"Ladies and gentlemen," he said, nodding to Edward as the one gentleman, "your host. May I present Señor Liam Murphy."

He stepped aside to reveal a beaming Murph, his blue eyes dancing just the way they had two evenings ago when we first met him in *The Cave*.

"Gotcha!" he said, moving toward us, arms outstretched to envelop each of us in turn in a great Irish bear hug. "I wish you could see the three of your faces! To be sure, I really pulled it off!"

"You didn't mention anything," I said when I finally found my tongue.

"And so I didn't darlin' girl. So I didn't. I hope you're not disappointed, then?"

"No, sir, not at all," Edward said at last. "Just surprised. I don't think any of us expected to see you this morning. Mr. Postman never mentioned this connection to me in our briefing before we left Cork Harbour."

"No," Murph said, heading over toward the coffee bar, "he wouldn't have. The two of us, we cooked up this little surprise for Jenn."

Another one. But before I could ask for a few missing details, such as why on earth Dad would find this amusing and what other things he might not have told us about Costa Rica and his connection to it, Murph was gesturing to us to sit at the white leather stools at the coffee bar while gesturing to the baristas to begin the tasting session.

They introduced themselves as Hector, Alejandro and Dante. They all had those smouldering, dark good looks that Latino men so often exude. There was a similar sexiness about each of them, although Dante had startlingly blue eyes to compliment his black wavy hair, unlike the deep brown pools of the other two. They all seemed to almost burst out of their white button-down shirts with the *Café Exquisito* logo on the upper left breast. Of course, that bursting would be via the muscles that were evident under the fabric. I thought I must be in love. They were all delicious, but Dante, with those eyes—well, let's just say that I had to make a supreme effort to focus on what they were telling us about the coffee.

Alejandro was laying out the tasting cups in front of us on the counter while Murph checked his phone messages.

Hector was meanwhile telling us about the history of coffee in Costa Rica in his deep baritone and lilting Spanish accent. Faith was drooling—I could see it. Edward seemed to be taking a dim view of Faith's drooling. So unprofessional, I suppose.

"The wonderful drink that we all know so well today arrived in Central America in 1740 and in our beautiful country in 1796. We began to export it to Chile, where the Chileans, with their audacity, shipped it to Europe and called it Chilean Coffee from Valparaiso. It was not. But today, we have recovered our brand."

I wondered what marketing program had granted him a degree because surely he had one!

Dante hadn't said a word yet but had begun to pour the deep brown liquid into the cups that were now in front of us. The smell was truly exquisite, and I was completely in agreement with the plantation's name.

"You first cup a hand over the mug to trap the scented steam," Hector said.

We all put our hands over the cups.

"A bit more like this," Dante said as he lightly placed his two hands over my own.

I was so surprised by this that I almost missed the fact that he sounded exactly like Valentina—the English accent with a touch of Spanish.

"Hey, Juan Val Dez, cut it out," Alejandro said, laughing.

My hands jerked away so fast Dante must have thought I was trying to slap him. His eyes clouded over momentarily, but the sparkle quickly returned. I was so startled hearing the name *Juan* that, at first, I didn't know who Alejandro was talking to.

"Who's Juan?" I said finally.

Dante laughed. "That would be me." He did a kind of formal bow, then, likely noticing my apparent confusion, continued. "That's what they call me. Juan Val Dez. Ever heard of him?"

Faith, who had been sitting quietly beside me, her hands over her tasting cup, finally joined the conversation. "Of course, we know who he is." She turned her head so that she was now looking directly at the side of my head. "Don't we, Jenn?"

I refused to turn my head to acknowledge her, but out of the corner of my eye, I could see her little smirk.

150

"Yes," I said, "everyone knows who he is. But why does everyone call *you* Juan Val Dez?"

Now, Murph joined in from his end of the counter. "I started calling him that when he was ten years old."

"*You* called him that when he was ten?"

"Yes," said Dante, "my father is a bit of a comedian, as I'm certain you have observed already. It's his Irish heritage."

"Your father?" Faith asked the million-dollar question before I had a chance to ask it myself.

Now it was Dante's turn to look confused while Murph's eyes danced in that mischievous way they had. "I may have forgotten to mention that I had another son. Not that it's relevant today, though, is it Dante? I believe we have a coffee tasting to conduct."

His tone was light-hearted, but I noted a definite directive in Murph's words. Back to work for his three baristas.

Dante nodded as Hector started to provide directions for the tasting. I could hardly concentrate as he began talking. I could see his lips moving, so I tried to catch a word here and there. All the while, my mind was reeling from meeting Juan—Dante. *Is it possible that he's really my Juan?* I was thinking. *Could he have written the note? If he did, did he expect anyone to find it? Follow-up on it? Obviously just a joke. Joke's on me.* This last thought was the one that dominated my monkey mind.

Now Hector—encouraged by Murph—was saying things like flavour, aftertaste and acidity. Then, all of the baristas were slurping in unison, and we were supposed to follow suit. I looked over at Edward, who was taking it all in – camera poised and filming this as if he were planning a National Geographic documentary. And Faith seemed mesmerized. *Is it the coffee or the baristas?* I wondered.

I slurped and sucked as best I could, trying to follow Hector's directions about what we should be tasting. It just tasted like terrific coffee to me. After we had all tasted three of the newest blends, I remembered to ask Hector if they had a sample of the one my father had requested.

"But of course," he said, smiling that wide, toothy smile. "We have many bags close at hand, as it turns out. Boss, may we take it from retail inventory?"

Murph nodded as he continued to savour his third cup of coffee. Everyone would be seriously hopped up before the day was over.

Murph then called over to Dante, who, by this time, was starting to stack the cups in the dishwasher behind the counter. "Do you have a moment to accompany Ms. Postman to the shop? She will tell you what she is looking for."

Dante stood up and smiled at me. "But of course!" It seemed that these baristas were nothing if not accommodating.

I followed Dante through a side door, leaving Edward and Faith chatting amiably over a cup of coffee. Their third? Fourth? I'd lost count.

Dante didn't say a word as we made our way across an incredibly beautiful courtyard. A quadrangle that seemed to be flanked on all sides by wings of the hacienda, the garden space was designed around a huge fountain that rivalled anything I'd seen in Rome. If I squinted, it looked just a bit like a miniature of the Bernini fountain — but not too miniature at that.

We entered the wing to the right of the one we had just left and emerged into what appeared to be a huge coffee boutique. I could hardly take in all of the coffee paraphernalia. The double-storey walls were lined with shelving right to the top – shelving that was brimming with coffee grinders, French presses, hour-glass shaped Italian moka pots, coffee makers of all sorts (although the single-serving types were prominent by their absence), espresso machines, coffee glasses, coffee cups, serving pots for coffee, decorative ceramics to hold your coffee beans and on and on. I had no idea there was so much in the line of coffee gear. Even as quickly as we went by the shelves, it was hard to ignore the number of items that bore the *Café Exquisito* logo. These people took their branding very seriously.

As I followed Juan/Dante down the aisles, I was trying to figure out how I could lightheartedly tell him my funny story of finding a note in the coffee shipment from his father's business without him thinking that this stupid woman had come all the way to Costa Rica thinking she might 'help' the hapless Juan.

I had just opened my mouth to broach the subject when we stopped abruptly in front of a gleaming coffee machine that had to be the most beautiful piece of electronic equipment that I had ever seen. It, too, bore the *Café Exquisito* logo proudly on the very front.

"Jenn – if I may be permitted to call you Jenn," Dante began. I nodded. I was seriously tired of all this Ms. Postman stuff, as if they were paying homage to me or something. He continued. "Jenn, I present to you the *Café Exquisito Series J One-Touch Cafeteria Sublime,* the world's most intelligent coffee maker."

I had to admit that it looked impressive—a combination of stainless steel and shiny chrome enhanced by a touch of black enamel. Of course, all of this was accessorized by an LED screen and its accompanying buttons and dials.

"After the best—there is nothing. You will forever after be spoiled."

As he said this, his eyes bore into me; I suddenly felt as if I were slightly unclothed. Were we still talking about coffee here? I almost hoped not.

"Ah, yes, it is beautiful," I said finally.

"But we are here to find you that bag of beans for your father. He does know that he did not have to send you all the way to Costa Rica to get it, did he not? Of course, I'm not complaining. I have been wondering about you."

He had been wondering about me? What?

I felt that the time had come. "Jua…Dante, I was wondering…I mean, there's kind of a funny story about my trip."

He was looking at me closely, all ears as far as I could tell. I walked over beside the table, groaning under the weight of mounds of coffee bean sacks and picked one up as if to demonstrate.

"Yes, funny story. I'm sort of working for my father right now." Sort of? Who was I kidding? I was most certainly working for him. Why I didn't want to come right out and say it is beyond me. I pressed on. "I actually work mostly on marketing and promotions—that sort of thing." I held the bag of coffee beans up to my nose and smelled it. I cannot even imagine what Dante must have been thinking of me at that precise moment. I suppose he thought I was a lunatic. But the story had to come out. I put the bag back on the display. "Anyway, I was working in my father's store one day. You know my father has a gourmet grocery store, right?"

Dante smiled. "But of course I know. How could I not know? Jenn, what are you talking about?"

"Yes...of course you know. Everyone here seems to know more about my father than I do."

"Why would we not know? Our fathers have been business partners for many years. Did you not know that?"

I didn't know that, and I told him so. I mean, how could my father not have mentioned this to me? Then it struck me. He probably had mentioned new ventures a few years ago, but I had a new job in the big city and was probably too caught up in my own life—and perhaps a wee bit disdainful of the small-town activities—to even hear him. He probably didn't press me with details that I wasn't interested in.

"To be completely truthful, Jenn, I didn't know anything about your father until I came home last year myself."

And so the story came out. Dante had been living in London and working for an advertising firm after finishing his MBA at Oxford. I was impressed. Then he lost his job. *Where in the world have I heard that story before?* I thought. He was forced to move home with his parents and take a job with his father, doing whatever his father wanted him to do. *Is there an echo in here?*

"So I guess I'm what you might call a boomerang kid." He picked up a bag of coffee beans and tossed it back and forth from one hand to the other. "Not so impressive a CV, is it?"

I started to giggle. Then I was laughing. I couldn't seem to stop. *Good lord, what must he think of me now?* When I finally was able to control myself, I told him my own sad story of boomeranging.

"What are the odds," I said, "that the two of us would meet under these circumstances?"

He was laughing now, too. When we finally calmed down, Dante said, "What was that funny story you were going to tell me about this trip?"

"Oh, that." I somehow felt a little less inclined to spill about the note among the coffee beans, but it did have to come out at some point. So I told him. But I did not ask him if he wrote it – if he was Juan Val Dez. I was too embarrassed at this point.

Dante looked puzzled. "You found a note? What did it say?"

I told him.

He walked over toward the window and sat down on a mahogany bench where customers could sit and admire the bounty. "Jenn, I wrote that note."

I was flabbergasted, and just a bit put off. Why ever would he have written a note suggesting that he might need help? My favourable impression of him, his personality, his CV—and yes, his looks—was beginning to fade.

"My father asked me to write it," he said.

I sat down beside him. "Why would he do that?"

"He said it was part of a marketing scheme. I thought it was meant to be found by a customer, and that customer was supposed to win something. He never did tell me the details."

"How could a customer have found it in a packing box?" I was really asking *myself* this question since none of this made any sense.

Just as I was trying to work this out in my head, Murph stuck his head around the corner of one of the shelving units.

"Well, you two, we were wondering where you'd gotten yourselves off to. Did you manage to find that coffee for your father, Jenn?"

I nodded and picked it up from beside me on the bench to show him.

His eyes twinkled a bit, and that little smile began to emerge. "Dante, did you happen to show Jenn the machine?"

"I did. Dad," Dante said, "we were just talking about that note you had me write to put in the coffee shipment a few months back for that marketing scheme. You never did give me any details."

"You didn't ask, son. I believe you had told me that you didn't need any details about anything since you weren't planning on staying." Murph crossed his arms and leaned against the shelves. He was still smiling — slightly.

"I might have said something like that," Dante said. Murph looked unconvinced. "Okay, I did say that, but now I'm more interested in details."

So Murph told us. He and Dad had cooked up the little scheme. Yes, it turned out that *Café Exquisito* was another one of my father's little business ventures that I had been too self-absorbed to pay attention to. He and Murph were partners not only in the *Casa* but also in the coffee production and export business. I felt very sheepish not to have known.

"Your father asked me to put some kind of a note in that shipment – I knew that it was destined for *Savoreaux*. He had some kind of a notion that you needed a wee bit of an enhanced business incentive, I think, was the way he put it."

"My father was behind the note?" My level of astonishment was beyond bounds at this stage. I felt like Alice in Wonderland.

"He said he'd arrange for you to be the one to find it. Seems he wanted to see if your curiosity could be piqued. He said your real dream was to be a novelist, and he wanted to see if this kind of mystery could spur you on to ideas."

I had no idea that my father was so devious — or concerned about my dreams. I thought back to the day I had found the note. Hadn't it been just a coincidence that I was the one emptying the coffee shipment that day — the day of the spider? Then I remembered that Dad had told me he had planned for me to do it later, but I was to take Ardyth with me to calm her down. Then I remembered his final admonishment that I should be the one to empty the cartons. He had known I would find the note. When I went to him with my scheme to come to Costa Rica, he had known why all along. I should have been angry with him, but I wasn't. I loved my father—and what's more, I knew he loved me despite my obvious self-absorption.

Dante seemed as surprised at this revelation as I was. Evidently, his father had kept him in the dark as well.

"Why did you tell me it was a marketing thing?" Dante said.

"Simply put, you were too busy feeling sorry for yourself for having to be in—what was it you called it? This godforsaken place—even if this godforsaken place and its inhabitants had taken you back in with open arms. If you hadn't spent so much time with your head firmly stuck up your arse, I might have been able to make you understand—to be a part of it. To be a part of any of this." Murph waved around as if to take in the entire plantation, then looked at me. "I'm sorry to lay out our family issues in front of a guest, Jenn. My apologies."

I shook my head, completely understanding. Dante and I were in precisely the same boat. I just didn't know how either of us was going to get out of it without falling overboard.

How to Know When You're in Love...and the Science to Prove It

Did you know that there are scientifically proven clues to know when you're in love? I do because I once had to write a lifestyle article for *Vivacity* on that very topic. I kid you not: there are people who research this kind of thing. And they get government grants to do it. I know because I interviewed three of them.

One of them was an anthropologist at Rutgers University who told me that there are thirteen signs, but I only remembered four. Feeling obsessed was one of them. Duh. That was a no-brainer, I thought at the time. Everyone knows that. I also remember that one of the thirteen signs was that people in love say that sex isn't the most important part of their relationship. In my view at the time, I thought that they all must be lying. The third one I remembered was that people who are truly in love will do absolutely anything for the other person. It seemed likely to me, but I wondered if that might get you into trouble. I also remembered the last one the researcher told me: that the spark always dies. God, that was depressing to be told that one of the sure signs you're in love is when it ends. Naturally, I thought about my own parents, who I just knew were still in love and flushed the whole interview. Pure bunk, I thought.

One of the other scientists I interviewed told me that one of the most important ways you know you're in love is when you start enjoying the same things that the other person enjoys—even if those things might have been a big bore to you before. Now, this one, I thought, has possibilities.

I was thinking about this the next day when I arrived on the pool deck to find Faith and Edward sitting at a table, glasses of lemonade at the ready, pouring over Edward's stock of books about Costa Rican flora and fauna. Now, this was not the kind of thing that Faith had ever even feigned an interest in before in her entire life. Faith was laughing and pointing, and Edward was more animated than I ever remember seeing him before. Faith just waved to me briefly and went back to her adoring attention. Had I been missing something?

Lest you think I had forgotten about Juan, be assured that I was on that pool deck at that very moment to tell Faith that I would be lunching with said Juan/Dante. As for being in love, well, I suppose I might have been a little smitten. It was hard not to be taken in by those dancing eyes and that sexy British-by-way-of-Spanish accent.

Anyway, Señor Mezza had the day off, so we were on our own. It turned out that Edward and Faith had plans to tour Manuel Antonio Park to see if they could spot any howler monkeys or sloths. Later, Faith had an appointment with Paloma. This trip was turning out to be much more eventful than I could ever have imagined. Yikes, I felt as if life were changing right before my eyes.

At precisely one p.m. (these Murphy people were nothing if not punctual), Dante pulled up in front of *Casa Exquisito* on an enormous motorcycle. I have never been a motorcycle aficionado, so I had no idea what make or model it might be; I only knew that it was large and loud—and unexpected.

"I hope you do like the open air, Jenn!" he said as he opened the seat to produce a second helmet meant for me.

Oh, I liked the open air well enough. Still, I remembered Faith once during her nursing education days when she had done a rotation on the transplant unit, referring to motorcycles as kidney-donating machines. Air I liked: it was these two-wheeled monsters that I was not at all sure I enjoyed. And I had no intention of becoming a Costa Rican kidney donor! How could I refuse to get on behind this hunky man and wrap my arms around his muscular torso, though? So, I did what the self-help books once told us to do: I faced the fear and did it anyway. I figured it would make a great magazine feature one day.

Dante carefully maneuvered the bike down the hill from the hotel and pulled onto the main road. Then he let it rip. I held on for dear life, trying to figure out what everyone who rode motorcycles saw in them. Did I mention I was terrified?

We sped along the roadway, passing tourists in rented vehicles (you could always tell), trucks loaded with coffee, and pick-ups moving farmworkers from one plantation to another. When we finally slowed down we were pulling into a lane and up a hill leading into what appeared to be an enormous farm. In the middle of the hill stood a single building that looked over what appeared to be a private beach and many miles away, the horizon. It was breathtaking.

"Here we are!" Dante said as he removed his helmet and shook out his hair.

"Where exactly is here?" I had hat hair so bad I thought it would never recover.

"Welcome to *Pablo's Place*."

And so it was. Pablo, it turned out, was an old friend of Dante's family. He had known Paloma since her childhood in San José, and when Dante introduced me to him as we crossed the threshold into the restaurant, Pablo enveloped me in a bear hug, the like of which I had never experienced. And he was, indeed, a bear of a man.

Standing at least six-and-a-half feet tall, Pablo resembled an ageing football player—the kind who are used as human walls on the defence. His greying hair was amiably mussed up, and he sported a large salt-and-pepper handle-bar mustache. He looked like the kind of guy you wouldn't want to meet in a dark alley at night, but his eyes told a different story. They danced and twinkled as much as Murph's did. Oh, and he seemed to think that Dante and I were a couple—a serious couple.

"We begin with a pitcher of Sangria," Pablo told us. "But you," he said, pointing a finger at Dante, "will drink but one glass.

I see that machine of yours out there. Your mother would never forgive me if I let you drink." So it would be up to me to hold up the side – the drinking side. And I do love a glass of Sangria in a beautiful setting.

We didn't even have to order. Pablo brought us plate after plate of what appeared to be Dante's favourite foods. In between enjoying the deliciousness, Dante and I got to know each other just a bit. He felt a bit responsible for my misunderstanding, although I told him he had nothing to apologize for. It had been a misunderstanding on my part but not on the parts of either of our fathers.

The most astounding thing was that Dante and I were essentially living parallel lives. Both of us had long lived away from home, pursuing our dreams. Both of us had lost our jobs without ever having considered that this would be a possibility. Both of us were boomerang kids. Both of us were working for our fathers and feeling like fish out of water. We had a lot to bond over. Amid all this similarity, though, there was one aspect where we differed.

Although both of our fathers had offered us entry-level jobs, Dad had never broached the subject of whether I should consider staying and working with him in the long term. He seemed to acknowledge that I had other fish to fry—other dreams to pursue. On the other hand, it seems that Murph wanted nothing less than for Dante to stay, learn the business and take it over in due course. And what a business it was!

Murph and my father together owned the hotel and the hacienda, and as if that were not enough, Murph also owned a hotel in San José and a resort in the north of Costa Rica in an area called Liberia. Dante protested his indifference to this business, but I could see that the idea wasn't as odious as the thought of staying in Cork Harbour was to me.

"It sounds like a huge company and a very successful one," I said, sipping on my third glass of the delicious, ruby-red Sangria.

"Yes. My father is a brilliant businessman—and my mother, a brilliant businesswoman. They have really done it together. It has been wonderful to see them doing it together over the years."

"Perhaps you'd consider staying?" I had no business asking him this since we hardly knew each other, but my tongue was loosened just a bit by this stage.

"I do love it here," he said, sounding a bit wistful, I thought.

"Then why not take your father up on his offer?"

"Jenn," he said, "look around. What do you see? Who do you see?"

I wasn't sure what he was getting at. I saw one of the most beautiful vistas that I had ever laid eyes on. *What's not to love*, I thought.

"You see tourists, Jenn, and no one else. How can I spend my life alone here?' He leaned across the table slightly toward me. "May I tell you a secret?"

I nodded, putting my glass down to lean in a bit closer. There was no one else to hear, though. We were on a private patio outside, overlooking the magnificent view. No one else was anywhere within earshot.

"Although I have never told him as much, I have always planned to come back to work with my father, but I had hoped it would be in my own time when I was ready. I had hoped to bring home a wife who would work with me as my mother has worked side-by-side with my father. They have been very happy, and I would like to have that kind of happiness in my life." He sat back and looked at the view. "I did not plan to return quite yet."

And this was his secret that I was not to tell his father. So, he did plan to return. He now found himself in the position of not knowing whether to stay now or go, to return later. It was quite a conundrum. For me, if I were able to get my act together and get a new job, I'd be back in the big city in a nanosecond—and my father was fine with that. However, I had to admit that I had never thought about what he might plan for the future of his own business. I'd have to make a note to ask him about that.

"You know, Dante," I said, "this is just a bit embarrassing, but one of the things I thought when I found the note and decided to come to see if I could find Juan was that I might be fated to write Juan's memoir. I thought it might be destiny. Crazy, huh?"

Dante looked at me thoughtfully. "Not so crazy. If one does not believe in destiny, what else is there?"

We spent the rest of our lunch chatting about all kinds of things: where we had travelled, where we would like to travel, books, movies, and our mutual disdain for much of what passed for social interaction in our generation. We even shared our Facebook profiles to underscore that last one. Then it was time to go.

Lunchtime had passed into the afternoon, and I wondered why Dante didn't have to get back to work.

"When I told my father that I was treating you to lunch, he insisted that I take the afternoon off. You are like family to him."

So, happy, sated and just a bit tipsy, I put that helmet back on my head and wrapped my arms around this gorgeous man once again as I slid onto the maroon leather of the bike's seat. As the wind blew by me on the drive home, I thought I caught a glimpse of what drew people to the open road.

Uncertainty: The Essence of Romance

The next week flew by in a series of day trips combining both work and play. Edward had researched several plantations where we strolled fruit groves and taste-tested a variety of fruits Faith and I had never heard of before. Some of them were not my cup of tea, after which I suggested to Edward that the fine residents of Cork Harbour might not be quite ready for all of them. One that we did like, however, was called *Marañon*. A curious fruit that resembles a yellowish-red, gourd-like apple with a green blob at the bottom, this fruit's flesh is sweet and slightly astringent, and its seed is the cashew. Did you know that if a cashew is eaten raw, it's poisonous? But roast it and, well, you know how delicious a cashew is!

We were also introduced to *zapotes*, *guanábanas* and *pipas* (green coconuts). In the end, Edward decided to begin shipments of at least two of the new fruits with the expectation that Dad's customers would be provided with ideas and recipes for their use. I think that's where I was supposed to come in so I had to gather as much information, recipes and general usage tips as I could like any good marketing coordinator might do. I even interviewed two chefs who used them in their signature dishes.

Señor Mezza also took us zip-lining at the top of the cloud forest—that was a magnificent experience that I will not be repeating as a result of my mild acrophobia. As I stood on the narrow platform in the treetops high above the floor of the rainforest, everyone else was marvelling at the sounds and the vistas. I, on the other hand, was hugging the tree. When I finally zipped my way to the end of the series of platforms and various treetops, I was proud of myself for doing it.

We also visited an iguana sanctuary, frolicked on pristine beaches and hiked densely treed parks. We dined with the Murphy family, and Faith holed up with Paloma for two days, doing whatever it was she was doing. Edward videotaped everything, and I thought a lot about the future. Then it was time to leave.

The evening before our departure back to San José and the flight north, Paloma and Murph hosted a dinner for us at the coffee hacienda. It was attended by the Murphy family, senior staff from the various Murphy businesses and assorted local dignitaries.

The hacienda sported an enormous function room, although the term function doesn't even come close to capturing the beauty of the room and the terrace onto which the tables, replete with snowy white tablecloths and sparkling crystal spilled.

When we arrived, I was escorted by Hector (who was so handsome in an actual tuxedo) to the head table, where I was seated between Dante and Murph himself. Faith and Edward were seated together at the closest table along with the dignitaries. Everyone took the formal dress seriously – Paloma had even managed to magically produce a tux for Edward and two fantastic dresses for Faith and me—although, to be fair, given Paloma's background and closet, this latter accomplishment wasn't really surprising.

When dinner was over and the requisite toasts had been made to the business and to us as the honoured guests, Dante excused himself saying he would be back shortly. Murph sat back down and turned to me.

"So, Jenn," he began, "how have things gone during your visit? How do you like us, this family of Irish-Costa Ricans?"

"My god, Murph, you have been wonderful. We have so much to take back to Dad. He'll be delighted with the work, I think."

"My dear, that's truly wonderful. Your dad is a great businessman – I should know! But," he said, sounding a bit more serious, "that's not really what I'm gettin' at, you know."

I didn't really have any idea what he was getting at and told him so.

"Jenn, my dear girl, we like you a lot."

Nothing. I had nothing.

"Dante likes you a lot."

"I hope so, and I like him," I said, taking a sip of wine. "We had a great time laughing at how much alike we are. Who would have thought?"

"Yes, indeed," he said, taking a great gulp of the Jameson Irish whiskey that one of the waiters had left there a few minutes earlier. "Jenn, if I may be so bold as to pry a wee bit, but how do you see your future?"

"Well, I'm going to do the best job I can for Dad while I'm in Cork Harbour, but the quiet life in Nova Scotia isn't really for me." For the briefest of seconds, I had this fleeting thought that I didn't know if it was the quiet life or Nova Scotia that wasn't for me – or even where those two ideas came from. "I'm going to start my job hunt in earnest after I finish this job for Dad. Then, as soon as I find a new job, I'm headed back to Toronto. In fact, I had a text from my former boss. I think she's into a new venture I need to follow up on."

It does sound as if you have a bit of a plan, then," Murph said thoughtfully.

I looked in the direction that Murph was now staring. He was looking at Dante, who had returned to the dining room and was now standing in the doorway chatting with Faith. He took another great gulp. "Jenn, how do you feel about Dante?"

"Dante? I feel fine. I…" Suddenly, I had a sinking feeling that I knew where this was coming from and, worse, where it was headed. "I mean, he's terrific."

"I know, I know. We all know he's terrific. But how do you *feel*?"

"Well," I said, carefully picking my words, "I feel that he and I could be great friends."

"Just friends?"

Just friends. I thought about the weight of his words. I remembered Faith once texted me a quote that went something like this: *Friends are people who know you really well and like you anyway.* It had made me smile then, and it brought a smile to my face now.

"Ah," he said, "you're smilin'. That's a good thing."

Uh-oh, what did he think I was smiling at? I glanced toward the bar where Dante had now stopped. He was laughing and joking with the bartender, a close friend of his. What, indeed, *was* I smiling at?

I looked around at the beautiful room, the laughing people, the exquisiteness of the surroundings. I heard laughter and chatter; I heard happy people. It was truly a magical place in the bosom of this wonderful Irish-Costa Rican family.

"Murph, I'm leaving tomorrow."

"I know, darlin', but there is no distance too far for true love to bridge."

Love? I hadn't said anything about love. I had just met Dante, and we hardly knew each other. Or did we?

"You know a famous Irish writer once said, 'The most important things in the world to do are to get something to eat, something to drink and somebody to love you.' If I might be permitted a fatherly bit of advice, perhaps when all three come together, you need to take notice."

"What did Dante say to you about me?" I was starting to hyperventilate just a teensy bit.

"Darlin', I think you better ask him yourself."

Dante was now heading back to the table with two glasses of champagne. Fortunately for our conversation, his way back was circuitous, and he had to navigate knots of people who wanted to chat with him along the way.

"The one thing I do know about my boy is that if he had someone here with him, he might stay."

I was stunned. I had thought that this had been Dante's secret. Could his father have known all along? An even more important question was this: Could he have somehow engineered this potential romance?

I turned in my chair and looked directly at him. "I thought you told me that Dad asked you to put that note in the coffee shipment. Was it your idea in the first place?"

He laughed. "You give me too much credit, love. I wish I had cooked it up with your father, but alas, I'm not that creative! No. But when you arrived, and I got to know you, I did hope that there might be a way for the two of you to find each other in all of this. You with your head for marketing, and Dante with his business sense. It would be a match made in heaven if you ask me." He was watching Dante as he was about to reach the table. "Well, at least for Paloma and myself."

"What about you and Mom?" Dante said, putting one of the flutes in front of me and one in front of his place.

"Nothing that would interest the likes of you, my son." Murph then drained his whiskey and got up. "Think I might have one more," he said, picking up the crystal glass. "See you both later. Do have fun."

This last remark was rather more pointed than I thought was necessary. Good lord, now I supposed that he wanted us to conjure up some kind of a romance. I looked at Dante as he set one of the flutes down in front of me. I was suddenly aware that my heart was racing, and my hands were so sweaty that I almost wiped them on the skirt of my silk dress, just catching myself in time to feel around on my lap for a napkin. I was remembering an article I had written for *Vivacity* once on the signs of the love-at-first-sight syndrome. Heart racing, breathing fast, sweaty palms, weak knees (okay, I was sitting down, so I couldn't really tell about the knees). *Uh-oh, am I in trouble here?* One of the characteristics that I also remembered, though, was the one that said people who are prone to the syndrome never develop feelings for a friend—it was either love from the start or it would never happen. Was Dante friend material?

"Jenn, your friend Faith is quite a woman. It seems that she and my mother are writing some kind of business plan together. What's that all about?"

"To tell you the truth, Dante, she's been a bit secretive about it. I don't know all the details, but Faith told me it was some kind of an online fashion business. I don't know much more than that." I had a sip of champagne, slowly savouring every drop. It was *Veuve Clicquot*, which, as you know, is my favourite!

"Well," he said, "they're as thick as thieves. And I must say I haven't seen my mother this animated about a project since she retired. It's good for her, I think."

Funny, I had just been thinking that it was good for Faith, but I didn't know what would happen when she returned home to James. I knew that she believed her marriage to be over and divorce inevitable, but face-to-face, things can be different.

"And what about that Edward guy?" Dante asked.

"Hmm? What about him?"

"He's a bit of a dark horse, isn't he?" I must have looked terribly puzzled, so he continued. "He seems a right nerd, but when you spend a bit of time talking to him, it's clear that he has quite a business head on his shoulders. Along with the photo genius, of course."

Of course. *What photo genius?* I was thinking. *And business head?*

Then, as if he could read my mind, Dante continued. "He showed me some of the shots he's been taking since he arrived. They're brilliant. I think they'll be terrific centrepieces for your father's marketing. I'm also going to suggest to Dad that he buy some of Edward's shots for the business here."

I was beginning to get the impression that Dante's passion for the business was, indeed, focused on this very business that his father wanted him to take over. I hoped that he'd be able to find a way to stay and be the next CEO. It would suit him.

"I must say they do make a terrific couple," he said, gazing languidly toward where Edward was sitting.

"Who makes a terrific couple?" It seemed I'd lost the plot a bit here.

"Edward and Faith," he said as if I should have known who he was talking about.

"Edward and Faith? They're not a couple," I said. "Good heavens, they hardly know one another."

Frowning, Dante looked at me. "I can hardly believe that. I've been talking to both of them, and it seems that they are quite in love."

I had just taken a small sip of champagne, which I proceeded to cough up all over the table in front of me. I grabbed my linen napkin and pressed it to my lips and then to the wet spot in front of me on the tablecloth. I took a breath and tried to compose myself. He had it so wrong.

"You are truly mistaken there, Dante. I don't think they've ever really spoken to one another before this trip except to discuss the comparative benefits of one vegetable over another. And since we've been here, I've seen nothing to suggest that they have any kind of a relationship beyond a mutual bonding over the intricacies of the camera."

"Well, Jenn, I hate to have to tell you, but you're wrong. Dead wrong." He sipped his champagne. "I think you have a blind spot when it comes to spotting love."

Okay, that was it. I would have to get back to him on that, but for the moment, I had now officially had it up to the teeth with being the only one who didn't seem to be in on the news. At least in the case of Edward and Faith, I knew he was wrong. But I was going to get corroboration anyway. I stood up. "I'll see you later, Dante." He looked a bit hurt, so I kissed his cheek, which brought a smile back to his eyes. "Later?"

He nodded. I knew that we still had unfinished business, but I had to find Faith. Right now. And talk to her about Edward. And Dante.

I made my way out across the patio, where guests had already left their tables. It was surrounded by tiki torches burning on its perimeter and flanking a set of steps that led to a water garden below. A small waterfall splashed gently into a pond where koi swam dreamily through clear water lit from beneath. It was the kind of scene that made you stop and take at least one deep breath.

I looked around to see if there might be another way back into the building when I heard soft laughter coming from what appeared in the moonlight to be a kind of conservatory right out of *The Sound of Music*. (Remember that scene where the oldest daughter sings *I am Sixteen Going on Seventeen* with her beau? Then Maria and the Baron get together later?) Then I heard a man's voice, and I froze. It was Edward, and if I was not mistaken, that little bit of laughter emanated from none other than my good (and clearly secretive) friend Faith.

"I think you better tell her soon," Edward said quietly.

I leaned forward, straining to hear like I've seen people do in the movies. It doesn't work. All I could hear were a few muffled words and then a rustling sound, as if someone were walking through the greenery. And the sound was coming toward me. I had nowhere to hide – or so it seemed. Frantically looking around and afraid of being caught eavesdropping, I dropped to the ground, crouching behind an enormous urn filled with bougainvillea, which flowed down the sides. They moved closer to the urn, stopping just beside it evidently to take in the night sky. *Good heavens! Couldn't they do that later?* I was getting a leg cramp.

I peeked around the urn as far as I dared, but all I could see was two hands – holding one another. They were holding hands. *What in the world is going on?* I thought. *The world has gone completely bonkers!* But before I had a chance to decide whether I would show myself or not, the decision was made for me because my bare legs started itching. I looked around. Immediately, it was abundantly clear where the itching was coming from. I was crouched in a sea of snow-on-the-mountain, a plant to which I am rabidly sensitive. If I stayed there a moment longer, I would not be able to wear bare legs for at least a month and the itching – well, I had to sit on an airplane in the morning, and that wasn't happening. As I jumped up, all I could think about was, *who would bring such an invasive plant from North America to Central America to punish the local gardeners?*

I must have popped up like a jack-in-the-box, judging from the startled look on both Faith's and Edward's faces. At that moment, I didn't care how it looked. My legs had started itching and burning so I, naturally, had started jumping around like a Mexican jumping bean.

Faith clutched her chest. "Oh god, Jenn. You frightened me!"

Evidently, I had not frightened her enough to have her drop Edward's hand, and he didn't seem inclined to let it go either.

"I think I've fallen into some snow-on-the-mountain! You know how allergic I am!"

Faith had now dropped Edward's hand and was looking at my legs with great nurse-like concern. No doubt she remembered the summer when I had discovered this allergy, and she had spent two weeks ministering to me as I lay in agony on a chaise lounge in my parents' back garden. I think that's when she decided to study nursing at university. Edward, of course, had no such memory.

"Jenn, for god's sake, what are you doing out here on the ground anyway?" he said.

I straightened myself up, still scratching as I did so. Glancing down, I saw that I had minimized the reaction by getting up as quickly as I did. By this time, Faith had determined that I wasn't in imminent danger of anaphylaxis. I had also had the presence of mind to wonder the same thing. What, indeed, was I doing?

"I was taking a walk," I said rather more petulantly than I had intended. I was naturally feeling a bit guilty, but I didn't want them to know that.

"You're stalking us," Edward said.

"I am not." I brushed some detritus from the hem of my dress. "And anyway, what reason would I have to stalk you?"

It was Edward's turn to look a bit sheepish.

Faith came over to me and put an arm around me—but it wasn't to console me; rather, it was to lead me unquestioningly toward a stone bench where she manhandled me into sitting down, then sat down beside me while Edward stood towering over us.

"Jenn," Faith began, "you're my best friend in the world forever. You know that, don't you?"

"Aren't we a bit old for that now?" I said, although in truth, I still used BFF in texts to her. Why was I being so crabby?

"I am just going to ignore that," she said, continuing. "You are my best friend, and I've been keeping a secret from you. Edward and I are..." She stopped.

"Are what?"

"Well, we're..."

Edward chimed in. "We're seeing each other, and it's serious."

In my experience, Edward had never been one to sugar-coat anything. He shot straight to the point. I tried to process this for a moment before I said anything. There was a palpable presence hanging in the air between us, and before I had an opportunity to gather my thoughts and respond, I was aware that the presence hanging in the air was the distinctive aroma of pot. Hash. Dope. Mary Jane. Grass. Weed. Well, you get it.

"What's that?" I said finally.

"What's what?" Faith said, thinking no doubt that I was referring to Edward's shocking pronouncement, which I was still considering.

"That smell."

"Jenn, you know exactly what that is, but it's not the focus of our discussion," Edward said, getting us all back on track. The pot party would have to wait.

And so it was time for me to be reminded that I was not the centre of the universe. While I had been navel-gazing and feeling sorry for myself back home in Cork Harbour, Faith had been engaging in a torrid affair with my father's second-in-command, a testament to her profound unhappiness with her husband. How could a good friend have been so blind? Further, it seemed that no one in the town knew about it, especially not James. The

173

husband is always the last to know, evidently. I didn't know how they had managed to keep everyone in the dark (especially me) even as we began to plan this excursion, but at least that explained why Faith had been so happy when Dad informed us that Edward was to come along.

"Of course, when your father told me about this tentative trip, I immediately convinced him that I should come along."

My eyes widened. "You were behind this?"

"Of course. And that's why I felt it necessary to be so particular about the research and the report I'll provide to your father." He didn't fool me a bit. Edward would have been just a particular, even if it hadn't been for this little bit of subterfuge.

It seemed that Edward and Faith had bonded almost a year ago over a certain shipment of avocados she had ordered for a Mexican fiesta she and James had been hosting for the medical staff at the hospital. When they had discovered a mutual interest in photography, there had been no stopping the chemistry.

I was beginning to see Edward in a whole new light.

"What happens now?" I said at last.

"My new business with Paloma?" Faith whispered.

"No. But we'll get to that later. What about you and James?"

"I already told you I had made a decision. I'm leaving him as soon as we get back to Cork Harbour."

"Are you planning to leave Cork Harbour?" For one selfish moment, I could picture the two of us sharing an apartment—me with a shiny new job and her running a new business.

But Faith looked puzzled at this. "Of course not. I love it there. I thought you knew that."

"What about Paloma and the business—whatever it is?"

She smiled widely. "That's the beauty of the web, Jenn. It's going to be a virtual couture shop. We're planning to specialize in made-to-measure wedding gowns embellished with hand-worked Costa Rican lace. She'll design and liaise with the lace-makers here. I'll get it up and running online, do the marketing and attract other designers." She smiled coyly at Edward. "Of course, Edward has agreed to do our fashion photography." She looked back at me. "I have a business plan, you know. I've actually been working on it for years, but I thought it was just a fantasy life. Now it's coming true!"

I had no idea how she planned to finance this venture, which seemed enormous to me, but that was a discussion for another time. By this time, the pot party was spilling out into the torch-lit outdoor space, and the revellers, including Murph and Paloma, were happily coaxing the band to set up for outdoor dancing. It was after midnight, but the night was young. To hell with that six a.m. alarm and early flight north.

When Life Gives You Reality, it's Time to 'Get Real'

Have you ever heard that dopey Dr. Phil and his 'get real' mantra? To tell you the truth, I was never really sure what this meant. I remember one time when Eleanor asked me to research a story on women who had 'gotten real' based on advice from Dr. Phil's books. I was able to find three women who would admit to following his pop-psychology approach to solving problems in their lives, and all of them ended up in worse situations. According to Dr. Phil, part of 'getting real' means confronting—honestly—other people in your life. I concluded that honesty in the form of complete disclosure might not always be the kind of reality that has a positive impact on your life in the real world. In the end, Eleanor thought that my piece was far too inflammatory and that it might just risk a lawsuit. She never did print it, but there has been a bit of the story that has stuck with me ever since.

I was thinking about this as I sat in my window seat, sipping on dubious wine and gazing distractedly out at the landscape 34,000 feet below me. I was thinking that what I needed at this point was some kind of real life. I'd had delusions of grandeur, it seemed. I didn't have a real job. I didn't have a real place to call home—you can hardly call your parents' basement home when you've been out on your own for as many years as I had. I didn't have a real relationship like Faith evidently did now. But I couldn't stop thinking about Dante. I had gone to Costa Rica allegedly to try to help someone who potentially was in trouble (sounds a bit foolish now, doesn't it), and ended up finding…what exactly had I found? A friend? My soul mate? *Where did that come from?* Had I found my life?

As I thought about all of this, Edward and Faith sat in the two adjoining seats to mine, amiably chatting and laughing softly at one another's stories. I think I was a bit jealous. That was unfair, I know. Faith had been fighting her own demons for some time, and now she had a few more battles to fight before she could move forward. More than anything, I was feeling unsettled by my own life.

By the time we had changed planes twice and landed at the airport closest to Cork Harbour (close is a relative term in those parts; the airport is, in fact, an hour-and-a-half drive from town), I had made a few decisions of my own. But before I could act on any of them, I first had to finish what I had started with Dad — after I confronted him about his dubious activities recently. I owed it to him to get this marketing project completed, but I could be making my own concrete plans as I did so. Then, I could deal with my curiosity about what Eleanor's new venture might be about. Maybe there was a place for me there. That said, I was wrestling with the feeling that any involvement I might have with her in the future would be a bit like going backwards rather than moving forward. Reality was beginning to sink in, so the first person I'd have to check in with would be Matt.

Throughout our trip, I'd had a bit of texting back and forth with Matt as you know, although I do find that texting is truly not a very good way to communicate. There is no such thing as a real conversation there, but I did manage to keep him updated on the oddities that presented themselves to me. What I had sorely missed was the chance to talk over all of the odd revelations with him. He's the sanest person I know in the world. We would need a seriously extensive conversation about the outcomes. Before I could even get to Matt, though, I was presented with yet another little twist. Dante had left several voice messages for me while I was in the air.

Dad had met us at the airport with the Range Rover, and we were now motoring our way home. With Edward in the front chatting with Dad, Faith and I sat in the back seat texting one another (I know—grown women and all, but in our defence, it would have been difficult to have any kind of conversation out loud with my father listening given the recent romantic revelations). As soon as we left the baggage carousel and made our way out to where Dad was waiting, Edward and Faith reverted to their pre-Costa Rica trip relationship to all appearances. They were merely acquaintances whose relationship was confined to the odd discussion of exotic fruits and vegetables. But I knew better, and I only hoped that Faith could get her marriage/divorce situation straightened out quickly before she became another bit of roadkill along the acrimonious marriage breakdown highway.

We dropped Edward off first. He lived down a private lane just outside the main part of Cork Harbour in a lovely little seaside cottage of sorts. One-and-a-half stories high, it was faced in stone and had a sloping roof with dormers. The chimney suggested what might have been a large stone fireplace inside. I was intrigued and, for a brief moment, considered the difference between this abode and the large, impressive one in which Faith now lived with James. Was she willing to give that up? Then, it occurred to me that this was, in many ways, a much lovelier place and way to live. Anyway, it wasn't my life.

Faith was next. Dad drove in along the circular driveway and pulled up in front of the stone steps. As we did, James appeared in the doorway and then proceeded down to the car to help Faith with her luggage. His face bore a kind of tight little smile that seemed so forced I thought his face might crack at any moment. Faith wasn't bothering with a smile; she simply looked stone-faced. James nodded at me when I got out of the back seat to sit up front with Dad, but he didn't say anything—not even 'hi.' As he turned to walk back up the steps to the door, Faith mouthed to me, "I'll call you." Then she disappeared into the house behind James, and the massive door closed.

"So Jenn, it's just you and me now, isn't it?" Dad said as he pulled out of the driveway and pointed the car toward home. "As

178

soon as we get settled in, I want to hear all about how Plan B worked out." He was smiling broadly as he looked straight ahead at the road. One might even say he was smirking.

And so, once I had unpacked my things in my basement room and checked my messages (there were three more voice messages from Dante and several texts—I smiled at one and laughed loudly at the others – he was so funny I had found), I made my way upstairs where Mom had prepared dinner. My little sister Emma was already at the table chattering on about some boy or app or text from some BFF or other. *God, had I been that self-absorbed at 18?* I had probably been worse. And I was realizing more and more by the minute that I still was. Well, at least she talked to her parents, which was more than it seemed many kids these days do. As for me, I had a long road ahead of me.

When dinner had been served, Dad raised his glass for a toast to a successful business trip, then turned to me. "So, Jenn, what have you learned that will be useful to you—or us?"

The question was more than a bit broad, and I had so much I needed to say, but most of all, I wanted to know why he had kept me in the dark about so much of his business, so I asked.

"The truth is, Jenn, that until you returned home, you never really showed any interest in my business. Murph and I have been friends and business partners for years, as you now know. It never seemed like the kind of information you'd be interested in."

"Why didn't you say anything when I broached the subject of a business trip to Costa Rica?"

"Because it was more fun this way." He sipped his wine while Mom began to clear the table.

I started to get up to help her, but she waved me back. "Emma will help. Won't you, Emma?"

Emma shrugged and glanced down at her phone before getting up to assist. Dad & I were alone in the dining room now.

"Did you really put Murph and Dante up to that note thing?"

"Yes, I did."

179

"Why?"

"Because I love you, Jenn, and I know that you're meant to be more than a marketing copywriter for a business in Cork Harbour. I know that you want more or at least different, but I wanted to see how curious you could be. I wanted to see if I could get you out of your comfort zone and really look at yourself and your future."

"Oh, Dad, sometimes I think I spend far too much time thinking about myself. At least, that seems to be one of the things I've learned over the past few weeks."

"Jenn, that's the most mature thing I've heard you say since you arrived back here."

Ouch. That hurt, and kind of puzzled me a bit. I had never considered myself to be immature, but now that Dad mentioned it, I began to think about how I might be coming across. I suppose when I really thought about it, most of the people I spent time with socially before I came back to Cork Harbour were just a tad immature – except Matt. He was the most mature thirty-something I knew. But none of us seemed to have achieved the kind of responsibility that my father and mother's generation had done by our age.

No one in my social group back in the city was married. Several were living with their significant others, but they hadn't made a long-term commitment. Several of them had even told me that they weren't at all sure about the longevity of the relationship. No one had children, and all of the responsibilities that this eventuality entailed. Try as I might, I couldn't even think of one friend who had a dog. There were a few cats, but you know that they require less hands-on commitment. No one owned a house. Most didn't even have cars. We didn't need them. We lived downtown and walked everywhere. We were all near thirty and answered to no one but ourselves. We had no responsibilities outside our working hours; no one even did any volunteer work. No one had time after yoga class, spinning class, the manicurist, the hairstylist appointments, the clothes shopping, the theatre evenings, the dinners out, meeting each other for drinks. My god, we were so narcissistic and immature, weren't we?

I was suddenly struck by the distinct feeling that I might be wasting my life. Maybe Dad was right: I did need a jolt out of my comfort zone. I just had no idea how that might happen. Or maybe I did. Plan B wasn't working out the way I had anticipated. At all.

How to Declutter Your Life

One of the first articles I ever wrote for *Vivacity* was about decluttering. I remember well the morning that Eleanor came into my cubicle waving a few pages she had printed off the internet. It was a report of a study by Princeton University researchers on the benefits of an organized and decluttered life. There was something in the results about how seeing a lot of clutter around you makes you unable to focus. When I chatted with Matt about this, he had vehemently agreed, based solely on his own anecdotal data. The truth was that he tried hard not to take the moral high ground on the issue of clutter. Still, his insane tendency to perfection in his own environment—both at home and at his office—resulted in his single-minded ability to focus on the task at hand and accomplish so much more than the rest of us managed. So, I did some more research and pounded out the article.

Along the way, I found a plethora of quotes and so-called truths about clutter. You've probably heard them: they're the kind of quotables that pepper your Facebook feed and sprinkle wisdom throughout your Twitter feed. They are usually posted by the more earnest and serious of your friends and acquaintances. I suppose they're meant to inspire us, but they just make me gag.

"The more things you own, the more they own you." Well, by the time I had arrived at the point of reconsidering my whole life, I had already gotten rid of most of what I had owned previously (except for that stuff I had stored in one of those storage spaces you rent by the month back in the city. Oops. Guess I hadn't really nailed that one yet.)

"Do something today that your future self will thank you for." I never really figured out what that one had to do with clutter, but maybe the thing you had to do had something to do with decluttering.

"Keeping baggage from the past leaves you no room for baggage in the future…" or something to that effect. Clearly, this refers to more than physical 'baggage,' but it does suggest that whichever way you look at it, you're going to have baggage. *sigh*

"As I unclutter my life, I free myself to answer the callings of my soul." Gag me with a spoon. The callings of my soul? Really? On second thought, maybe I should listen. Listening to that inner voice would have to wait, though. My immediate 'callings' were from my cell phone. And they were from Dante.

We hadn't spoken in the past two days, so when I finally was able to clear a time that I could be alone holed up in my boomeranger hideaway in the basement with no interruptions, I texted him to tell him I'd be available for a face-to-face-but-online chat. I was mindlessly surfing through online magazines and had just spied something interesting when my computer pinged. Dante wanted to talk. I clicked 'accept,' and there he was: his handsome face filling my screen. I could feel my pulse quicken just seeing him there. I glanced behind me in that flash you get just as you realize that the background might be untidy, unattractive, too much information, incriminatory or all of the above. It seemed benign enough.

"Jenn, how wonderful to see your face. I was worried."

"Nice to see you, too, Dante," I said. "Why were you worried?"

"Since you left, there is so much to tell you. Things that can't fit into a text message."

I had left only two days before. How much could possibly have happened in that length of time that was earth-shaking?

"I'm all ears," I said, settling back into my chair.

"First," he began, "I have missed you. I don't think I had a chance to tell you how much I enjoyed meeting you."

"I enjoyed meeting you, too, Dante."

"Jenn, I've made a few decisions. It seems that Dad somehow knew that what I really want out of life, at least eventually, is to live in Costa Rica and run his business. I'm not sure how he knew."

"I think our fathers know us better than we think, Dante. Maybe even better than we know ourselves."

"Yes," he said. "Well, as you know, he is right. But I told you that I was concerned about finding my soul mate."

Where is this going? I was thinking. *Calm down, Jenn,* I told myself.

"Jenn, would you consider coming to Costa Rica and working here? We need a new marketing director, and you could have time to write. I know that you would come to love it here."

Good lord, he's offering me a job.

"Dante, I'm flattered. I truly am, but I'm a big-city kind of girl. And as much as I complain about it, I really do love winter."

"Jenn, I don't seem to be expressing myself very well." He stopped for a moment. "I'm in love with you."

My mouth actually dropped open, but no sound came out. Had I heard him correctly? He could not have possibly just said he was in love with me. Or could he?

"I know it's sudden, Jenn, but I've always believed that when I met the right one—my soul mate—I'd know. And I know. You and I are meant to be together. Remember our conversation about fate? It was fate that brought us together. We shouldn't fight it if we want happiness in our lives."

Fate? It was my father who brought us together. Fate had so little to do with it. Or did it? Maybe Dad was the instrument of fate—or whatever.

I could feel my eyes starting to fill with tears, and this was not at all what I wanted. But in that moment, I realized that what I did, who I was and perhaps even more importantly, what I did in the future had an impact on others. I was not the centre of the universe – not by a long shot. I had affected this lovely man, and truth be told, he had deeply affected me. I now knew this.

"Dante, you are one of the most lovable and interesting men I've ever met in my life. I do want to get to know you better, but this is so sudden that if either of us were to make a final decision so quickly, we might both live to regret it. Don't you agree?"

"Is that a 'maybe'?" He smiled just a little.

"That's a let's give it a go," I said, and for the first time in my life, I felt that I knew where something was going. There were going to be obstacles—all those kilometres came immediately to mind—but is there ever anything worthwhile in life that doesn't have obstacles?

We then spent an hour just chatting and getting to know one another better. At the end of the conversation, we agreed to talk weekly and keep one another updated on our lives in the short term. The longer term? We'd have to see.

How to Change the World: Or at Least Your Own World

For the next two months after the Costa Rica adventure, I put my nose to the grindstone to focus on helping Dad with a new marketing campaign that was intended to enhance his international presence. I hadn't learned a lot about marketing in grad school or through my previous job at *Vivacity*. Let's face it: I learned nothing about marketing. But when it came to developing a plan for my father's business, I found that I had a kind of innate sense of both his target market and the kind of messages that would resonate with them. What's more, I found that I was absorbed in it, loving the possibility of getting people to spend money on Dad's products online. I know, I know. Marketers aren't considered the most ethical and forthright business people in the world. Their sole job is to get you to believe that you need something that you had no idea you needed or wanted until they tell you that you need and want it and are willing to buy it. It supports the consumer society that's always being vilified. But in my defence, Dad's livelihood depended on it, and I truly believe (don't laugh at me) that people who bought his products would actually enjoy life more. Now, you can't argue with that, can you?

I also spent a good many evenings binge-watching *Mad Men*. I had never laid eyes on the show before but thought that if I were going to pursue this marketing thing, I should know from where this twenty-first-century activity emerged. I fell in love with the wardrobe and a little bit with Don Draper. When he said, "People want to be told so badly what to do that they'll listen to anyone," I knew that I'd found my mentor. He also said, "Success comes from standing out, not fitting in," but I don't think that was original. I didn't care. I thought it was brilliant.

American satirist P.J. O'Rourke, whose books I devoured in grad school, once wrote, "It is better to spend money like there's no tomorrow than to spend tonight like there's no money!" It was always my mantra when I had money flowing in – it certainly had no problem flowing out when I was ensconced in the middle of a big city whose myriad activities twinkled at me from every street corner. "Buy me!" "Eat me!" "Drink me!" and on and on. It was like Alice in Wonderland – she seems to be a recurring motif in my narcissistic deliberations about myself. Now, though, the work I was doing was becoming more important than the money.

Dad didn't pay me very well by marketing standards, but I was beginning to realize that it didn't matter. It was a little like studying for another graduate degree: I was learning so much from the work itself, not to mention my father, who, as I knew, was a wizard of a businessman. He patiently answered the myriad questions that popped into my head regularly and pointed me to other resources—even a few of his old marketing books from his MBA. Many had stood the test of time, it seemed. I also did my own research. I downloaded several current marketing books, voraciously devouring everything I could find. Throughout this process, I was in regular contact with Eleanor who was indeed onto a new project. She was creating a network of online retailers for women. An extension of her original idea of *Vivacity*, it was to be a kind of clearinghouse for vetted places for women to shop for everything from books to cosmetics to wedding gowns. In fact, it was called *Vivacity Atelier*. It was this issue that I planned to discuss with Faith on the occasion of our first dinner together three weeks after our return. But, before we could get to business issues, I had to check in with her on the social scene.

"Are you seeing Edward these days?" I began.

"Sshh," she admonished me, looking around to see if we were being overheard. "No, we decided to step back until I could straighten out the mess that is my marriage."

"How's that going anyway?"

"James is furious and wants us to go to counselling. I don't want counselling. I know what I want, and it's not a second chance with James." She twirled a forkful of pasta and popped it into her mouth. "I've been to see Calista, you know."

Calista Taylor was a high school classmate who had gone away to law school and then returned and set up practice with her father: Taylor and Daughter, LLC, the business was called. It doesn't fall off the tongue as easily as Taylor and Son might, but it's a feminist victory in a place like Cork Harbour. We all just need to get used to it!

"How is Calista, anyway?"

"She's fine. Just as straight-laced as she always was, but I think she's a great lawyer. Detail-oriented, you know, and she's got a lot of divorce experience."

It was true. Calista had cornered the market on family law, specifically divorce law, in our little town, where this business was surprisingly active. I had once thought that Cork Harbour was our own little Peyton Place (remember that fictitious town? It was a place in a 1950s novel where incest, lust and adultery reigned supreme). I couldn't remember any incidences of incest, but lust and adultery we had in spades. Calista had a fabulous house she had bought all by herself and a country club membership to prove it. Faith's divorce was probably in good hands.

"How's Edward?" she asked, sipping on her glass of Barolo. "I miss seeing him."

I still had trouble seeing the two of them together – they seemed to live in two different worlds, but Faith was my best friend, and if he made her happy, that was enough. "Working hard. I think Dad's planning on giving him a promotion."

Faith beamed. "How wonderful. He does so deserve it, you know. He's brilliant. I can't wait to discuss my business plans with him. I hope to have the big D over with before he starts taking photos for us."

"Speaking of business plans," I said, "how are things going?"

"Oh, things are really getting off the ground. Paloma and I talk every three days and I have four designers about to sign on."

"About that," I said, "my old boss Eleanor is into some kind of a business where she's grouped online retailers for women into some kind of a network for better access and presumably pricing."

"Not *Vivacity Atelier*?" Faith had put her fork down and was now sitting up straight.

"Yes, that's it. She's been hinting about a job for me doing her 'content creation' for their websites, blogs, and other stuff."

"Are you going to take the job?" Faith said, excited. "I've been reading about her new venture, Jenn. It's going to be wonderful. If we could get our business onto that network, we'd have a real shot."

"First, she hasn't offered it to me in so many words yet. Second, that's what I wanted to talk to you about. If you're interested, I could put you in touch with her."

Faith squealed in delight. I hadn't seen her that happy since prom. It was almost like old times – almost. I still had the little issue of my uncertain future in front of me.

Three weeks later, I was hard at work in my little cubicle (Dad had partitioned off a bit of quiet space for me by this time) when my phone rang. It was Eleanor who wasn't in the habit of telephoning anyone without a preliminary text to announce her intention.

"Oh, Jenn, I'm just delighted to have found you. I hope I'm not interrupting anything."

"Eleanor, I'm so happy to hear your voice. How is everything in Toronto?"

"That's why I'm calling you. I hope you know that you were one of the best writers I ever worked with in all my years as a magazine editor."

I was not aware of that, but it was terrific to hear it.

"Anyway, you know I've been hinting to you that you might consider joining this new venture of mine. I'd like to formally offer you a job as head of content creation for the network." She stopped for a moment and I wasn't sure if I was supposed to chime in yet.

Here it was at last! My opportunity to leave Cork Harbour (again) and return to Toronto. Matt would be so excited. I was so excited! Why, then, was I unable to utter a single word? Too overwrought with delight, I supposed.

"Jenn? Are you still there?' she said. "I know this might be rather sudden, but I'd need you here in three weeks. Things are moving along very quickly, and by the way, I never did thank you for sending Faith and Paloma along to me. Paloma has agreed to be the face of *Vivacity Atelier*! We are all so excited and need to capitalize on this as soon as possible."

"Eleanor, this is... uh...wonderful for you."

"And for you!" she said. "We'll build this together, and you'll be able to do what you do best: write!"

Why was I feeling a bit off balance by this? It was exactly what I'd been waiting for. Eleanor was offering me the opportunity to return to Toronto and to work with her, a boss from whom I had learned so much in the past. Then it hit me. That was just it: *it was in the past.* I couldn't go back; I needed to move forward. The trouble was that I was still looking forward to a future that was out there in the mist. I needed desperately to find appropriate windshield wipers so I could see through it clearly.

"Jenn? Are you still there?"

"Yes, Eleanor, I'm still here. This is a terrific offer..."

"Then why am I not getting the message that you really feel it's terrific?" she hesitated for a moment. "A bit like going backwards, isn't it?" she said softly. She always had been the most perceptive person I'd ever met – after my father, that is.

"Eleanor, if this had come up six months ago, I would have jumped at it. You wouldn't have been able to hold me back. But now – well, I'm still figuring out a few things."

"You know, Jenn, Andy Warhol once said something that I always thought useful in my life. He said, '*They always say time changes things, but you actually have to change them yourself.*' I've followed that my whole life, and I'm willing it to you as your new mantra. I know you'll find your place in the world, but if you ever decide to do a bit more writing of the kind I'm talking about, I'll always have a place for you in my organization."

Until that precise moment, I didn't realize how much I really loved this woman. I loved her from the cat's-eye tips of her rhinestone-studded reading glasses to the tips of her very well-pedicured toes.

We chatted briefly for a few more minutes, then agreed to keep in touch. When I hung up the phone, I felt a kind of lightness that had eluded me for some time. I sat myself down in front of my computer and started writing. Before I knew it, two hours had flown by, and Juan had materialized on the pages of what appeared to be a book about a Costa Rican immigrant family in Toronto. I had characters. Now, all I needed was research material – a lot more research material.

The next two months flew by in a flurry of writing, research, dinners with Faith, Skype calls with Matt and Dante (but not both at the same time, although each one wanted to meet the other), and enough ideas to fill two journals. Matt's longstanding advice about that freelance career seemed to have taken root at last, and I had successfully queried several magazines and sold the following articles:

✓ *How to be the Best Boomerang Kid Ever* (This was a bit of a self-indulgent memoir, but it paid a few bills, and I am something of an expert now. I even interviewed my parents.)

✓ *Exotic Fruits Passions: What Your Choices Say About You* (Okay, this one does look a bit like the stuff I wrote for *Vivacity*, but you have to start a new career from somewhere, and Edward was a font of information for background.)

✓ *How to Deal with an Overbearing Husband* (Faith put me up to this one—I didn't ask her to be my silent source; she actually suggested it. I think her 'interview' with me was a bit of talk therapy for her as she moved ever closer to divorce.)

Obviously, I was busy!

It wasn't long before my father began to ask me how much longer he could expect his marketing director to continue to be available since her writing career seemed to be advancing. My mother then started making noises about the basement room, and I knew it was time to get back to being an adult—or becoming one for the first time.

Putting on Your 'Big-Girl' Panties Might Be the Best Thing You Ever Did

There are lots of funny quotes about becoming an adult – about growing up. Most of them seem to bemoan adulthood. For example, I'm sure someone on your Facebook list of so-called friends has put up something like this: "I've put a lot of thought into it, but I don't think being an adult is going to work for me." Or maybe, "Being an adult is the dumbest thing I've ever done." Or even, "I miss being the age when I thought I would have my shit together by the time I was the age I am now." Well, now, whenever someone posts something like this, I just feel sorry for them. They are missing this whole adventure of actually taking responsibility and being that adult, being the grown-up in the room.

So here I am. I've been back in Toronto now for a year – yes, a whole year, and so much has happened.

I finished the draft of my first novel. I haven't found an agent or a publisher yet, but I'm not sure it's ready to see the light of day yet, anyway. That freelance career has really been working out well, though, and pays the bills. I can't afford the kind of apartment I had before, and I'm not as far downtown as I used to be, but since I don't run out to bars every night, it's just fine by me.

A month after I got back to the city, I was on the subway heading down to the waterfront to take in the sights and sounds of a summer afternoon and soak up a bit of urban atmosphere. Sitting across from me was a family of four. They weren't saying much to one another, and I wasn't sure that they spoke English.

The husband and wife looked a little scared, but their two little girls—perhaps four and six—were more wide-eyed than frightened. The woman's headscarf, combined with their lack of comfort with the subway, suggested to me that they might even be recently arrived refugees from some war-torn part of the world. God knows there were so many places, and the families needed a place to live. As I was thinking about this, one of the little girls, a little dark-eyed beauty, began staring at my face. I smiled at her.

She tilted her head slightly and pointed to my nose. "What that?"

I put my finger on the tip of my nose. "Nose?"

"What that?" she said, pointing to my ear. She had sidled over closer so that she was now sitting on the seat beside me. Her mother looked slightly panicked.

"Ear." Then I had the game. I pointed to my arm. "Arm."

She said, "Arm," and started to giggle.

And on we went from one body part to another until the train pulled into Union Station, and we all got off. I waved to the little girl. "Goodbye!" I said.

"Goodbye," she repeated, mimicking my accent.

As I walked along the boardwalk later, this scene kept repeating itself in my head. She wanted to learn English. That much was clear. When I got home, I started researching opportunities to teach English to immigrants and the next thing I knew, I was helping out at a school where they had taken in a large number of refugees. I was an English tutor to seven little girls, all of whom were so hungry to learn my language. I was smitten.

Lest you think I had turned into some kind of perpetual do-gooder, you need to know that I never lost my love of shoes, although it's safe to say that my current position—work-at-home freelance writer—did not require much more than T-shirts and yoga pants as work attire. I did, however, try to provide a good example for the little girls when I met with them twice a week.

Faith and James were divorced in due course, and after a respectable month (!), she and Edward picked up where they had left off upon our return from Costa Rica. Faith's business venture was soaring: she and Paloma were featured as cover stories in *Chatelaine* magazine only last month. I'm only sorry I didn't have the foresight to pitch that one myself. *Chatelaine* pays better than most of the magazines I've been writing for lately! Anyway, when I opened my mail yesterday, there was a handwritten invitation to Faith and Edward's wedding, so I'm off to Cork Harbour in two months to see them married and presumably living happily ever after.

Faith had told me that James's most persistent argument against divorce had been, "What will everyone think?" Of course, no one in Cork Harbour gave a darn about their personal life, despite what he might have thought. He, however, didn't buy that, so he decamped for Halifax, where he took a position on the faculty of the medical school. He doesn't make quite as much money now, but he doesn't work as hard, either. And Faith is delighted that he no longer bumps into her at every turn.

And speaking of weddings, on Saturday I'm going to a wedding. Matt made partner in his law firm and met the love of his life all in the same week. David is a lovely man who, as Matt likes to say, fluffs pillows for a living: he's an interior designer and is just about the nicest, kindest person I've ever met. Of course, they have a killer apartment—not that Matt's wasn't always wonderful, but it now has that professional touch. Their wedding is in a private dining room at the Four Seasons Hotel on Saturday, and I could not be happier for him. I do love a chance to get dressed up once in a while.

As for Dante and—we are in close touch on a weekly basis. He is still working for his father, and I have a trip to Costa Rica planned for next month. To tell you the truth, I cannot wait!

Oh, just a minute. The buzzer is ringing.

~

~

~

~

~

Oh. My. God. Dante is here. I wasn't expecting him. When I answered the door, his voice boomed from down in the lobby, and my heart started thrumming madly. I stood by the door until he arrived and when I opened it, there he was, pulling a small suitcase behind him and holding out his hand. In that hand was a blue box—a blue box from Tiffany's. Tiffany's!

It sparkles. A lot. Every time I move my hand, it sparkles.

I guess *Plan B* did work out. In the end.

About the Author

Patricia J. Parsons has written over twenty books, including health and business books, a memoir, two historical novels, and women's fiction. She has been a fashion design and sewing fanatic for most of her life, a passion she writes about online at The GG Files at gloriaglamont.com. She lives, writes and sews in Toronto.

- Connect with her on Instagram @patriciajparsons
- Join her on Facebook @patriciaparsonswriter and at facebook.com/groups/12dresses
- Visit her website at www.patriciajparsons.com

Other Books by P.J. Parsons

The "almost-but-not-quite-true" stories
The Year I Made Twelve Dresses (Book 1)
Kat's Kosmic Blues (Book 2)
The Inscrutable Life of Frannie Phillips (Book 3)
Something I'm Supposed to Do (Book 4)
This is the Way the Story Ends (Book 5)
It All Begins With Goodbye (Book 6)

Plan B (lit-for-intelligent-chicks)
Confessions of a Failed Yuppie (lit-for-intelligent-chicks)
Something More Than Love (historical fiction)
Grace Note: In Hildegard's Shadow (historical fiction)

All titles are available on Amazon and other online sites.